Bliss was totally outraged

"You have no rights over me whatsoever!" she hissed.

"While you're in Peru, you're under your brother-in-law's guardianship. He has passed that guardianship to me and—"

"Now just a minute!" Bliss was having great difficulty keeping her voice down.

But Quin Quintero, her newly appointed and most definitely unwanted guardian, wasn't giving her so much as a minute. His voice was every bit as aggressive as hers as he told her bluntly, "And since it seems that you—willfully and stubbornly—refuse to take my advice—then you leave me with only one course of action."

Do your worst, Bliss wanted to fire back, but knowing him, she didn't doubt that he would.

Jessica Steele first tried her hand at writing romance novels at her husband's encouragement two years after they were married. She fondly remembers the day her first novel was accepted for publication. ''Peter mopped me up, and neither of us cooked that night,'' she recalls. ''We went out to dinner.'' She and her husband live in a hundred-year-old cottage in Worcestershire, and they've traveled to many fascinating places—including China, Japan, Mexico and Denmark—that make wonderful settings for her books.

Books by Jessica Steele

HARLEQUIN ROMANCE

3041—FAREWELL TO LOVE
3065—FROZEN ENCHANTMENT
3077—PASSPORT TO HAPPINESS
3095—UNFRIENDLY PROPOSITION
3114—HIDDEN HEART
3126—A FIRST TIME FOR EVERYTHING

HARLEQUIN PRESENTS

725—GALLANT ANTAGONIST
749—BOND OF VENGEANCE
766—NO HOLDS BARRED
767—FACADE
836—A PROMISE TO DISHONOUR

FLIGHT OF DISCOVERY
Jessica Steele

Harlequin Books

TORONTO • NEW YORK • LONDON
AMSTERDAM • PARIS • SYDNEY • HAMBURG
STOCKHOLM • ATHENS • TOKYO • MILAN

Original hardcover edition published in 1991
by Mills & Boon Limited

ISBN 0-373-03156-4

Harlequin Romance first edition October 1991

FLIGHT OF DISCOVERY

CHAPTER ONE

IT STILL seemed incredible to Bliss that she was actually here in Peru! She had arrived in the capital, Lima, yesterday and her enthusiasm was as total as it had been at the start. She showered and began to get ready for dinner in her hotel, her thoughts on how, thanks to her dear sister and her sister's husband, her visit to Peru had been made possible.

A stray wisp of conscience tugged when she thought of how she really ought to phone her sister, Erith, and tell her that she was here in Lima. Swiftly Bliss turned her back on the idea. Her sister had only been married for two and a half months and, in Bliss's view, was still on her honeymoon. In actual fact, she recalled without effort, Erith and her husband had planned a three-month honeymoon cruising in one of the luxurious yachts which Dom, Erith's husband, had designed and built. But it was no surprise to Bliss, having heard Erith go into raptures about her husband's home in Jahara, that they should want to get back there. For Jahara, the place where Dom had his hacienda, had pulled them both and was the reason why they had cut short their cruise, deciding to continue their honeymoon at the place they both loved.

Bliss's eyes grew dreamy as her thoughts flew back to nearly four months ago. She had been at home with her father and stepmother, recovering from a particularly nasty bout of double pneumonia, and Erith had gone to Peru to find out more of what was happening to Audra, their stepsister. The trip to Peru had been deemed necessary when their stepmother had received but one letter only, one very worrying letter at that, in all the six months her daughter Audra had been living there.

Bliss, who owned to having more than a passing interest in archaeology, would have leapt at the chance to go. But she had not fully recovered from her fatiguing illness when the decision had been made that someone of the family should go after Audra.

'It's not on for you to go, love, it really isn't,' Erith had told her gently when, despite feeling below par, she had been gripped by just the very idea of perhaps treading where the Incas had trod.

'But, Erith . . .' she had tried to protest anyway, her large green eyes unconsciously pleading.

Erith had the same large green eyes and long Titian hair, and they shared the same pale, quite stunning complexion, and Erith's tone was warm with love as she regretfully told Bliss, 'No buts, love—we wouldn't rest a minute if you went.'

So it had been agreed that Erith must go to Peru, and Bliss was to discover that it was just as well—in more ways than one—for she'd had a set-back in her convalescence and had landed up back in bed again.

She had pretended that she felt much better than she had done when Erith had had to go, and was indeed starting to pick up again when some days later they'd received a cable from Erith saying that all was well with Audra. Shortly afterwards, with Bliss back again on the road to recovery, they had received the most exciting phone call from Erith. Exciting because, as well as telling them that Audra was already on her way home, Erith, a new note there in her lovely voice, had gone on to state that she would be coming home herself the next day—and that she would be bringing with her a very special man!

Excitement had given way to total jubilation when, on the heels of Audra, Erith arrived with the handsome Peruvian she had fallen in love with—Domengo de Zarmoza. From the first it had been plain that Erith and Dom had eyes for no one but each other, and Bliss had not needed any telling that but for their stepmother—whom both she and Erith loved—Erith and Dom would have invited them out to Peru, and would have been married without further delay in Dom's country.

But, with their stepmother being a very poor traveller, and with Dom impatient to marry Erith, it was three weeks later, at the little village church at Ash Barton, that the two were married.

'You'll come and see us at Jahara,' Erith had urged Bliss as the two hugged before the elder sister by one year went away.

'Try and stop me!' Bliss had exclaimed—but she had not thought it would happen so soon.

Not that she would be going to Jahara yet, Bliss mused, as she came out of her reverie to realise that she had showered and donned fresh underwear and a soft green silk evening trouser suit, all without knowing it.

A smile curved her lovely mouth as she thought back to how, two weeks ago, on her twenty-second birthday, she had received the gift of an open-dated return flight ticket to Cuzco, via Lima. Cuzco was the nearest airport to Jahara, Erith and Dom had told her in their accompanying letter, but since she had been so ill they were enclosing sufficient funds for her to rest overnight at a hotel in Lima before she continued her journey. They had included the name of a hotel—an expensive one, Bliss guessed, if she was meant to spend all that money on just one night's accommodation.

With the flight ticket being undated though, it was left to her when she used it. But that they had sent the ticket at all meant that they were not averse to her dropping in on them. It was a fact, Bliss remembered thinking at the time, that she wouldn't mind being somewhere else other than Ash Barton just then.

She owned then that she'd had the devil's own luck just lately. For she'd barely returned to her job at the library when, not having once been out in all weathers on a dig or having done anything to earn it, she had caught a summer chill. Naturally, having had so much time off recently, and despite her father and stepmother's protests, she had gone to work. Though not for long. She had been feeling quite dreadful and had been, without being fully aware of it, on the point of collapse when her boss had suddenly noticed that she looked ready to drop.

He had suggested he drive her home. 'This time,' he'd said as he'd helped her out of his car, 'don't come back until you're really well.'

She had been making good progress in her recovery on her birthday morning, and a shade reluctantly, she had to own, she had allowed Ned Jones to take her for a drive. Her reluctance stemmed, she knew, from the fact that while she had thought Ned more of a friend than a 'boyfriend', he was starting to show signs of being 'keen'.

Things had come to a head that night when he'd driven her back to her home and had tried to make a meal of kissing her. 'For goodness' sake, Ned!' she exclaimed, and, feeling not the faintest flicker of anything for him other than irritation just then, she had politely thanked him for taking her out and had gone indoors.

It was during that night when, restless and sleepless, she realised that she wouldn't at all mind getting away for a while. Ned had taken to calling at the house uninvited, and, now that her irritation with him had faded, she realised that she didn't want to hurt him. He had been a good friend while she had been laid low, so it seemed more than a little unfair to her mind, even though he had shattered the bounds of friendship with that kiss tonight, that now that she was feeling so much better she should suddenly tell him that she didn't want to see him any more.

Yes, she decided, she wouldn't mind at all being away just now. Excitement started to grip her as she thought of the birthday present she had that day received from Erith and Dom and suddenly—even though she spent many minutes afterwards working it all out—she knew that her decision to go to Peru was made.

Naturally, since she thought of her sister and brother-in-law as still being on their honeymoon, she had no intention of intruding. She would at some time call in and see them, of course; not to do so when she was in their country would be extremely rude— besides which, she missed Erith still and wanted to see her. Not just yet, though . . .

Bliss spent the rest of that wakeful night in working it all out. Firstly, there was her job to consider. Officially, with Dr Lawton being sticky about her returning to work this time, she was still on sick-leave.

To her way of thinking, though, he must soon, if not this week then certainly next, be bound to say that she was fit enough to return to work. Since her boss, however, was insisting that she didn't show her face in the library again until she was in tip-top condition, would he think she'd got an awful cheek if she tacked her unspent holiday allowance on to the end of her sick-leave and took off for Peru for three weeks? Knowing Mr Barnham, she felt sure his good wishes would be hers.

Next Bliss thought about money to finance her adventure—hotels and the like—but she could foresee no problem there. Her father and Jean, her stepmother, had given her a sizeable cheque for her birthday and since she'd been ill on and off for the last four months she had spent barely any of her salary. She had her savings too, she remembered, recalling how she, Erith, their father and Jean had pooled all their resources in order to afford Erith's trip to Peru in search of Audra. A gentle smile curved Bliss's lovely mouth as she thought of how, with overwhelming charm, her brother-in-law had pointed out that since they had been so generous in finding the money to send his adorable Erith to him they must allow him to repay every penny.

Dom, who apparently was quite wealthy, had wanted to make things generally financially easier for them, in fact, and had spent a long while in private discussion with their father. But it was Erith who had told Bliss that Dom would like to make her an allowance.

'But I don't need it, Erith,' she had told her. 'Dom's already insisted I take back the money I put in the kitty—anything else would be taking advantage.'

'I told Dom you'd say that!' Erith had laughed, and in love, and because she was so happy, she had hugged Bliss from pure joy.

Bliss was unsure how her father and stepmother would take her decision to go to Peru as soon as she could get everything arranged, but, feeling financially quite affluent, she told them her decision over breakfast the next morning.

'Will you be well enough to go by then?' her caring stepmother fretted.

'I'm fit enough now,' Bliss asserted with a kind smile, having had quite enough of being treated like an invalid.

'You'll let Erith know the date of your arrival, of course,' her father chipped in, causing Bliss, who had no such intention, to search for ways not to tell him an outright lie.

'I'll let her know the moment I know myself what time I'm due in Cuzco,' she assured him—and two weeks later she departed England's shores and headed for Peru.

And here she was, Bliss thought sunnily as, silk-trouser-suit-clad, she left her room and made her way down to the hotel's restaurant. The head waiter saw her at once as she entered the dining-room and with a beaming smile he at once came quickly toward her.

'Good evening, *señorita*. Where would you like to sit?' he enquired, the admiration in his eyes as he stared at her hair and pale complexion unmistakable—for all he seemed to be doing his professional best to hide it.

'Where I sat last night will be fine,' she replied without thinking, and was about to remind him where in the large dining-room she had sat—because he couldn't possibly have remembered—when, to show that he had clear memory of where the Titian-haired English woman had sat last night, he led the way over to the exact table.

'Thank you,' she smiled, and was left by herself to study the menu.

Then, 'Good evening, *señorita*,' said another voice, and she looked up to see it was Señor Videla.

'Good evening,' she responded warmly, having spent a very pleasant hour or so the previous evening in conversation with him and his friendly wife in one of the hotel's lounges.

Bliss still had a pleasant smile on her face for Señor Videla, a fairly good-looking man in his late twenties, when a much taller man of about thirty-five or so strode into the dining-room and, clearly a man who scorned the use of head waiters, opted to find his own table.

His direction brought him striding nearer to Bliss who in moments was recognising that there was something aristocratic and authoritative about him also. Nor was that all, because he was just level with her table when Señor Videla enquired, 'Have you the objection if I share your table, *señorita*?'

His phraseology caused her smile to widen. 'Of course not,' she replied, but she found, as some sort of a grunt of disgust came from the dark-haired man who was passing by, that she was looking not at Señor Videla, but straight into a pair of slate-grey eyes. Slate-grey eyes which held the coldest look she had ever seen.

In the next moment, as her smile faded and the man strode on with a decidedly arrogant expression, Señor Videla took a seat at her table and Bliss suddenly knew what that grunt of disgust had been all about. Whatever nationality the slate-grey-eyed man was, one thing was for sure—the man understood English. That being so, on hearing Señor Videla ask if he could share her table he had assumed—not having seen her in Señor and Señora Videla's company last night—that Señor Videla was trying to pick her up! Clearly too, from her smiling reply of 'Of course not,' he'd thought she was agreeable to being picked up!

For a few fuming seconds Bliss felt like getting up and going over to the lordly swine's table and asking him who the devil he thought he was to look down his nose at her.

Then, as from the corner of her eye she saw him take a table some way away, she decided that she wouldn't lower herself. So instead she looked across the table to Señor Videla and, having been acquainted last night with the fact that the Videlas' three-year-old son was in hospital in Lima recovering from surgery on an ear problem, she enquired how the little boy was.

'He is healing well, but has much tears today,' Señor Videla said, and smiled.

'Oh, I'm so sorry,' Bliss sympathised, and Señor Videla smiled again.

'Manco want to go home, but cannot and so is giving his mother the hard time,' he revealed, and Bliss wanted to say once more that she was sorry, but he was going on in his quite good English, 'Which is the reason for my wife to say she cannot—er—impossibly—show her face in the restaurant tonight.'

'She's been crying too?' Bliss compassionately guessed.

'She is much brave, my wife,' Señor Videla told her
proudly. 'Not until we left Manco did she show that
he was breaking her heart—since we left him, until
she fell asleep a half-hour ago, she has not stopped
crying.'

Bliss made sympathetic noises, really feeling for the
couple who were being torn apart over the unhap-
piness of their three-year-old. From then on, as they
ordered from the menu, they conversed pleasantly
until, the meal over, they made to leave the restaurant
at the same time.

She had been quite pleased to have Señor Videla's
company during dinner, and there was a smile on her
face as she turned back to the table for her shoulder-
bag. Her smile abruptly faded, though, when her
glance flicked to the other side of the room and, as
if guided by some homing device, she found that she
was looking straight into the slate-grey eyes of the man
who had looked down his nose at her earlier. His
expression hadn't warmed, she observed as she
switched her gaze from him. Quite obviously he was
now of the opinion that, having dined with a man
whom she'd never seen before until he'd paused at
her table, she was now off to have a high old flirty
time with him. Well, let him think what he likes, she
thought crossly, and, aware that Señor Videla was
courteously waiting, she picked up her bag, and went
with him from the restaurant.

At the lifts, after tendering warm wishes for his
family, she left Señor Videla and went up to her room.
She quickly forgot Señor Videla, however, and, as she
began to think of what she had planned for tomorrow,
she very soon forgot the cold-eyed individual from
the restaurant who clearly either had a down on

women, or had taken an instant dislike to her—and her 'fast' morals.

Bliss was up bright and early the following morning with her sights set on visiting the recently unearthed fifteen-hundred-year-old Royal Mochica tomb some four hundred or so miles from Lima, which was said to be richer in gold than the tomb of Tutankhamun. In any event, as Bliss took a short plane ride that would take her most of the journey, she knew that quite a bit of the gold brought out from the tomb had been sent to Germany for storage.

She was hopeful, however, as she exchanged a plane for a vehicle to take her over the rough track to the Moche archaeological site. If her information was correct there were relics to be seen from Lord of Sipán's tomb, in the nearby Grunning museum at Lambayeque.

Everyone whom Bliss bumped into that day was most helpful, and having spent so long at the monumental site, which extended over two acres, that she almost missed her return flight, she arrived back in Lima with her eyes ashine from her pleasure.

Her pleasure had in no way dimmed when, after a quick shower, she changed into a neat red dress that should have clashed with her hair but which miraculously didn't and went down to dinner.

For the first time, with so much buzzing around in her head, she missed having someone to talk to. It would have been super if she could have discussed with some like-minded person the Peruvian archaeologist Walter Alva's discovery of the burial place of the warrior-priest.

But there was no one, not even Señor Videla. Not even, she found herself thinking, *him*—he of the arctic slate-grey eyes. Though heaven forbid that she should ever want to spend time in conversation with *him*!

Holding down the impulsive urge to ring her sister Erith, Bliss finished her solitary dinner, thinking that perhaps the Videlas had checked out. Perhaps, with luck, *he*—old slate-grey eyes—had checked out too. Proof, however, that the Videlas had not checked out was soon apparent when the first people she bumped into in the hotel lobby were Señor Videla and his wife.

'Hello,' she greeted the happily smiling pair brightly, and, because they looked so happy, she ventured, 'You seem cheerful.'

'We are,' Señora Videla sang. 'Manco is coming out of hospital tomorrow, and we can go home.'

'Why, that's splendid!' Bliss beamed, and spent a few minutes in conversation and then, wishing them well, bade them goodbye.

While Señora Videla made for the few shops in the hotel complex in search of some gift for her son, Bliss made to go in the direction of the lifts. It was then, though, that she had evidence that the man with the icy grey eyes had not checked out either. For, with Señora Videla already a few steps away, her husband suddenly seemed to remember a little of his mealtime conversation with Bliss the previous evening, and delayed following his wife to enquire, 'Did you enjoy the Sipán site today?'

'Oh, yes,' Bliss exclaimed enthusiastically, her eyes at once ashine again—that was, until she suddenly noticed the glacier-eyed man who chose that very moment of her seeming to be in private, smiling conversation to walk by. Their glances connected. He looked through her. She looked through him. 'But you mustn't get me started on the subject,' she told

Señor Videla as his wife took a couple of steps back to join them, 'or the shops will be closed before I finish.'

Bliss had another splendid day the following day, though she did not have to travel so far, but with her journey only ten miles or so this time she was able to go by taxi. Her trip that day was to another recently discovered site, the site of El Paraiso, which was dated about two thousand years BC and was a pre-ceramic site over which experts were still arguing. Was it temple or domestic architecture?

She returned to her hotel and was certain that if the experts didn't know for sure then she most definitely could not give an opinion.

She knew as she went down to dinner that she wouldn't see the Videlas; it would be pleasant, she thought drily, if she didn't see *him* either. Why the icy-eyed man should have rooted in her mind as *him* she had no idea, but she quickly ousted him, and, feeling most decidedly hungry, remembered that she had forgotten all about lunch, and quickly chose from the menu.

She had left the dining-room and, again resisting the temptation to ring her sister, she strolled through to one of the shops selling picture postcards, and selected a few to send home.

She was walking away from the shops and towards the area of the lifts, and was studying the picture postcard she had treated herself to of the gold and turquoise *tumi*, the ancient spade-like ceremonial knife, when suddenly she cannoned into someone.

Someone who clearly knew she would not comprehend any of the Peruvian languages before she so much as opened her mouth, she realised as a curt,

'Why the hell don't you look where you're going?' assaulted her ears.

In the split second before she regained her balance and looked up, Bliss had a fair idea just who the owner of the voice was. She was not mistaken! She flicked a glance upwards and met full on the icy blast of slate-grey eyes. She did not have flame-coloured hair for nothing.

'And why the hell don't you learn some manners?' she erupted hotly, and, uncaring if she knocked him over—though, for all he was without spare flesh, he was too powerfully built for her slender form to have that much success—she brushed past him and, too angry suddenly to wait for the lifts, she made for the stairs. Really, when she had come across no end of nice people in Peru, why was it constantly her misfortune to keep coming across *him*?

CHAPTER TWO

BLISS'S equilibrium was restored by the morning. She had discovered that there was a wealth of museums, historic churches and houses in Lima, so she was up early and anxious not to miss a thing.

The sky was overcast, however, and more cloud entered her day when, dressed in cream corduroy trousers and matching jacket, she went in to breakfast. It was early still, so it was no wonder to her that no one, bar one person, was down to breakfast. But why did that one person have to be *him*?

He feigned not to have seen her—for all she knew he had from the flicked glance he took in her direction—and she feigned the same. Oddly, though, as she seated herself with her back to him, she found that she had total recall of everything about him, from his well-groomed dark hair and clean-shaven firm chin to his immaculate business suit and whiter than white shirt. She could even remember seeing his briefcase propped up on a chair next to him, she realised with some surprise. She then forcibly ejected him from her mind, and a smiling waiter hurried over to her.

'Forgive me, *señorita*,' he apologised abjectly, 'I did not hear you come in.' He cheered up, however, when Bliss favoured him with a sunny smile.

Just in case she again forgot all about lunch that day, she ordered a cooked breakfast. She was tucking into scrambled eggs and ham when, briefcase in hand, *he*, without a glance, strode past her table.

Have a terrific day, she thought sourly, and wondered why a man whom she knew not the first thing about should, when her thoughts were usually pleasant, have such an acid effect on her. He'd have a terrific day, anyhow, she considered; he was that sort. Quite plainly he was off to some business meeting—perhaps he wouldn't come back.

On that happy note, Bliss poured herself another cup of coffee and decided that, since the first museum she wanted to visit didn't open until nine, the church La Merced, which had been established in 1534, before the founding of Lima itself in fact, would be her first port of call.

Bliss spent a full if tiring day, and returned to the hotel at half-past five having been so absorbed by her visits to several museums that, apart from a stop for a cup of coffee, she had again missed lunch.

She was in good spirits, however, as she waited for the lift. Her good spirits momentarily plummeted, though, when as the lift arrived another guest appeared from nowhere and as the lift doors opened, he—with his briefcase—stepped into the lift with her.

Bliss was still cursing her misfortune that it didn't seem she could turn around without finding him there—a slight exaggeration, she owned—when, 'Number?' he rapped. Plainly, he was impatient for her to tell him the number of her floor so that he could start the lift in motion as soon as possible and thereby reduce the length of time he was forced to be incarcerated with her.

Bubbles to you! Bliss fumed, and, ignoring him, she shot out a hand and stabbed at the button she required.

'Manners!' he tossed icily down at her, and Bliss had to stand there and accept that, as she had last night accused him of having none, perhaps he had been right to bounce that accusation back at her.

The lift stopped. She got out; so did he. She went one way; he went the other. It was a large hotel. She prayed she had seen the last of him.

Bliss let herself into her room, put down her bag, and owned to feeling pleasantly tired. She had just taken off her watch as a preliminary to going to take a shower, however, and had placed it down on a bedside table, when the phone the table also accommodated suddenly pealed for attention.

'Hello,' she said on picking it up, and, with delight and not a little astonishment, she heard and recognised her sister's voice.

'You were just going to ring me, weren't you?' Erith queried with mock severity.

'Erith!' Bliss exclaimed. 'How lovely of you to ring—but how on earth did you know that I was here?'

'Dom took a guess that you'd be in the hotel we recommended when I put a call through to Dad, and he said you'd left England almost *a week ago*!'

'There's so much to see,' Bliss said quickly, starting to feel a trifle guilty that maybe she should have given in and telephoned her dear sister some days ago. 'How's Dom?' she asked.

'Wonderful,' Erith murmured softly.

They had a long conversation in which Erith relayed that their father and stepmother in England were well, and Bliss related what she had been doing since her arrival in Peru. Then Bliss was asking how things were going with Erith in her new life, but could hear in her sister's tone before she said anything at all about

the terrific man she had married that Erith was sublimely happy.

Which, by the end of their conversation, had
stiffened her resolve not to intrude on their honeymoon. Which in turn caused her to have to be quite
firm when the feeling that she would like very much
to see Erith again tried to intrude. Firmly she held
down that feeling when her sister told her that she
and her husband would meet her at Cuzco airport
tomorrow.

'Actually, Erith,' Bliss got in quickly, 'I'm not
coming to Cuzco tomorrow. I'm——'

'But Bliss——'

'In actual fact,' Bliss hurried on, already sensing
that her sister, who had been very protective of her
since their mother had died some ten years ago, was
not going to be easily put off, 'there's so much I want
to see here first.' At just that point Bliss felt a tickle
in her throat and was forced to break off to cough,
and then swallow, before she went on, the swallow
unfortunately not quite soothing the tickle, 'I'll come
and see you, of course I will, but first I thought I'd
go to Arequipa—and if it's at all possible I must get
to Nazca.' She broke off, annoyingly, to cough again.
But before she could continue Erith was speaking
again—and sounding quite alarmed.

'You're not well!' she exclaimed. 'You've been
overdoing it. You've caught a chill again——'

'Erith!' Bliss burst in on a laugh, and finally said
goodbye to her sister, having had to spend quite some
minutes in convincing her that she was perfectly well.

A warm smile played around her mouth as she went
and poured herself a glass of mineral water and, taking
it with her, she slipped off her shoes and went to relax

on her bed while she sipped the water until the annoying tickle went from her throat. She placed the glass on the side table, but stayed with her long legs stretched out on her bed. If she was tired, the tiredness was worth it for all she'd seen that day, she reflected as for the next hour she remained where she was as she renewed her strength, and thought pleasant thoughts, mainly about Erith and Peru, as she dipped in and out of her memory.

Her thoughts were again on Erith when about an hour and a quarter after her phone call the phone rang again. Must be getting popular, she thought drily, having occupied the same room for four days now and having not heard so much as a peep out of the phone until now.

'Hello,' she answered as, phone in hand, she wondered what this call would be about.

She was not left wondering for long. It was her sister on the line again, but Bliss's pleased surprise changed to total astonishment when Erith told her the reason why she was ringing her a second time.

Apparently her concern about her when she'd put down the phone from their previous conversation must have shown in her face, for her husband had wanted to know what was worrying her. And, having got from her that she was a shade anxious over Bliss, he had taken over. The upshot of which was that, acquainted with the details of their conversation, he had at once contacted a friend whom he knew to be in Lima. Bliss's expression was incredulous when, not believing any of this was happening, her sister went on to tell her that Dom's friend of long standing would call on her to see if there was anything he could do to ease the path for her in any way, shape or form.

He would, if she mentioned it to him, help her arrange her flight to Arequipa, if she'd like him to.

'Erith!' Bliss protested, when she'd got her breath back. She'd managed to make her own flight booking when she'd wanted to get to the Royal Mochica Tomb—though it was true that the desk clerk downstairs had been most attentive in his assistance. Her sister, however, seemed to think that she was protesting on another front.

'You've no need to worry, Bliss,' she said quickly. 'Dom wouldn't ask just anybody to check if you're all right.'

'I know that!' Bliss replied, appreciating her sister's concern, but not too thrilled at the idea of Dom sending someone to check that she was all right. 'I didn't mean . . .'

'Don't be difficult, love,' Erith coaxed, and caught at Bliss's conscience who was suddenly appalled that at this happy time for dear Erith she, inadvertently, was the one responsible for putting a cloud in her sky.

'So, what's his name?' she asked, brightly. 'And do I have to stay in all day tomorrow waiting for him to ring?'

'You're lovely when you're not being obstinate,' Erith told her, but to Bliss's ears she sounded much relieved and back to her former happy self when she told her, 'Dom calls him Quin, but he'll probably introduce himself formally as Quintin Quintero. He comes from an old aristocratic Peruvian family,' her sister went on, to fill in some of his background as if to show what a highly esteemed man he was.

'He lives in Lima?' Bliss questioned, wondering if she could get away with asking for his phone number and telling her sister that she would ring him if she needed her way smoothing in any area. But already Erith was denying that he had an address in Lima.

'He's an industrialist with factories there and, because he believes in supporting local industries too, he owns a fish meal plant on the coastal region where he lives,' she was informed. All very laudable, Bliss was sure, but that still left her kicking her heels tomorrow waiting for him to get in touch. 'Dom was at university with him and trusts him implicitly,' Erith went on as though wanting to impress on her that she too could trust him equally implicitly.

'Does he speak English?' Bliss asked, resigned by then to the fact that if she didn't want to upset her honeymooning sister she was going to have to go along with what she had arranged.

'He did his postgraduate year at Oxford, Dom tells me,' Erith replied, and Bliss noticed that there was a special warmth in her sister's smiling tone each time she voiced her husband's name.

What could she say? 'I'll look forward to meeting his friend,' she murmured, trying her best to sound sincere when—with every minute precious—she visualised spending the whole of tomorrow hanging about waiting for him to ring her. 'Will he contact me in the morning, do you suppose?' she hinted.

'He'll contact you tonight,' Erith laughed, clearly knowing her better than Bliss realised. 'He's taking you to dinner.'

Bliss put down the phone, having been informed by Erith that Quin Quintero had suggested he could call for her at eight. She picked up her watch, saw that she had plenty of time to get ready, but then followed through her earlier intention of going to have a shower.

At ten to eight, she was dressed in a sedate dress of deep lemon, and had by then realised that as this man Quin Quintero had been at university with her brother-in-law, he was in all probability the same thirty-six years old that Dom was.

Not that it mattered if this man Quin had been a student of mature years in his university days, she mused. She looked in the mirror to make sure that the small amount of make-up she wore was all right, and that her long Titian hair needed no more attention, and then realised that she had started to feel very much better about everything.

She'd be eating anyway, wouldn't she? So it was no hardship to dine with the aristocrat Quintin Quintero who, from the sound of it, was a pillar of society. She would convince him, of course, that she had no need whatsoever of his help, but, really, it had been super of her brother-in-law to go to the lengths he had on her behalf.

When the hands of her watch showed that it was exactly eight o'clock, Bliss anticipated that someone would ring from reception any second now to tell her that a Señor Quintero had arrived and was waiting for her. When her phone stayed silent, however, but about a minute later someone knocked on the door of her room, Bliss realised that Señor Quintero had obviously asked reception for her room number and had come up to her floor to collect her personally.

She had a smile on her face as she went to answer his knock. She opened her door—and her smile abruptly disappeared. The fact that the expression on the face of the tall, slate-grey-eyed man who stood there rapidly altered too did not impinge on her then as, 'Yes?' she demanded curtly, a second before harsh, cruel light began to dawn. Then, 'Oh, no—not *you*!' she exclaimed.

'I don't believe it!' he retaliated, and looked absolutely appalled.

Bliss bridled—some people she knew would be glad of the chance to take her to dinner. 'You're not...' She broke off, then rephrased it, 'Are you Quintin Quintero?' she demanded.

'It's true, then,' he grunted.

'What's true?' she questioned belligerently.

'That you're the female who is—and I quote—"sweet, gentle, and with a pleasing personality" whom I've come to take to dinner.'

Bliss tilted her chin a proud fraction higher. 'Thank you for calling, *señor*,' she told him arrogantly, and didn't miss the glint that came to his eyes at her uppity tone. 'But consider your duty done. I wouldn't go to dinner with you if——'

'How old are you?' he sliced through what she was saying to grate.

'Twenty-two,' she found herself replying—when she'd no such intention.

'Then act your age!' he snarled.

'Act my...?' she gasped astonished.

'Stop being childish and be grateful that your brother-in-law——'

'Ch-childish...!' she spluttered.

'Your brother-in-law, not to mention your sister, is concerned enough about you, your health, your delicate——'

'My health!' Bliss burst in hotly, having determined some while ago that she had done with being ill. 'There's nothing wrong with my health!' she erupted on a point of honour as, standing toe to toe, she glared at the stony-expressioned Peruvian.

Unspeaking he looked down his aristocratic nose at her for some seconds. Then, suddenly, a mocking light had come to his eyes. 'Is there nothing wrong with your appetite either?' he drawled, and, all at once, Bliss was wary. Somehow, now that his anger had gone, she didn't trust this mocking side to him.

'What do you mean?' she questioned bluntly, hostilely.

He shrugged. 'You want me to ring your sister and tell her we didn't dine together because you weren't feeling hungry?'

Bliss felt her mouth actually open in her surprise. Of all the... She got herself together and was quite ready then to tell him to go and phone away—and then she remembered how terror-stricken Erith had been when she'd gone down with pneumonia, how she'd nursed her and coaxed her appetite back. And Bliss hated Quin Quintero, because he had the upper hand—and seemed to know it.

'That's blackmail!' Bliss stormed angrily, sparks flashing in her eyes. Too late she realised that she had entrenched his blackmail hold on her further by confirming for him that she didn't want her sister to worry about her. She *should* have told him to do his worst, she realised belatedly.

'That's me keeping my word about what I said I'd do,' Quin Quintero told her toughly, his mocking mood not remaining long, she noticed. 'Look,' he said, plainly not afraid of offending her feelings, 'I'm as reluctant to carry out this—hand-holding—exercise, as you are to participate.' Hand-holding! She almost erupted again. 'But,' he went on to lay it on

the line, 'Domengo de Zarmoza is a very good friend
from way back—and I've assured him that as you are
now a member of his family it would be my pleasure
to dine with you and to put myself at your disposal
should you have any problems.'

Bliss reckoned she had only one problem—*him*. But
she could see from the set of his jaw that she either
went with him and allowed him to keep his promise
to his friend of some years or he'd get on the phone
to Dom straight away. Which would result, she saw,
starting to feel thoroughly fed up, in Erith having
nightmares, and might see the pair of them inter-
rupting their honeymoon to fly at once to Lima to
check in person that she was well.

'It's ridiculous!' Bliss snapped, but, because she had
no other option, she tightened her grip on her bag,
and, moving out into the corridor, she secured her
door.

Without another word being spoken they walked
side by side to the lifts. It *was* ridiculous, she silently
fumed. She didn't want to dine with him, he didn't
want to dine with her, but what were they doing?
Going to dinner together?

Her opinion had in no way changed when, Quin
Quintero obviously deciding they could eat in the same
hotel where they were both booked in, the lift stopped
at the restaurant floor, and they both stepped out.

They were seated in the dining-room and were well
into their first course before either of them addressed
the other again. Then suddenly Bliss became conscious that Quin Quintero was studying her. Swiftly
she raised her head and saw that his eyes were on her
flame-coloured hair.

Abruptly, he took his eyes from her hair, and, his tone unhurried, he seemed to think he should ask, 'Do you need assistance in any matter, *señorita*?'

'None, thank you, *señor*,' she replied politely, if coolly, and returned her attention to her soup.

Their second course had arrived, and she was cutting into her steak when he murmured suavely, 'I trust you didn't have to renege on a promise to dine with anyone else in order to dine with me.'

For all of a second, Bliss fixed him with a straight look from her large green eyes. You swine, she thought, knowing full well from his icy disdain, not to mention his look of disgust when it had appeared that she was allowing Señor Videla to 'pick her up', that he was having a dig at her.

But she'd be damned if she'd explain her passing friendship with Señor Videla and his wife, so instead, and without batting an eyelid, she replied sweetly, 'I had no other offer for tonight,' and left it to him to work out that if she'd had a better offer then she sure as hell wouldn't be dining with him.

Which, she soon saw, he had instantly done. Why his mouth should suddenly start to tug up at the corners as though her barely veiled reply had amused him was beyond her. Not that his mouth did break out into a grin, or anything like it, she observed before she took her glance away from what she all at once realised was a rather nice mouth.

Any hint of a smile had been sternly repressed, she observed when next she looked at him. Oddly, then, when she just knew that she wasn't even passingly interested, she found that she was questioning, 'How about you, *señor*, did you have to cancel any long-standing arrangement in order to keep your promise to my brother-in-law that you'd dine with me tonight?'

Quin Quintero surveyed her for long moments down his straight nose. But although from the arrogance of the man she knew that he was thinking scornfully, Would I? all he replied was a short, 'No.'

And, when it shouldn't have done—for she was doubly sure that she wasn't the slightest bit interested—his terse monosyllabic answer peeved her. 'Ah,' she said as the reason why he had no other date that evening suddenly dawned. 'You're married!' she suddenly declared.

'I assure you, *señorita*,' he replied stonily, 'that I am not.' There was something in his tone that warned Bliss that she was treading on very sensitive ground here.

Which, when she had always been instinctively most careful of other people's feelings, made it all the more amazing that she should hear herself state, as if knowing it for a fact, 'But you've come close to getting engaged—and recently.'

Oh, my word, she thought, when Quin Quintero gave her a withering look as though to enquire what the hell had that got to do with her. Though to her amazement, he did, contrary to her expectation, deign to answer. 'For a while one of us believed it would come to that,' he clipped, his look defying her to say another word on the subject.

'Which means,' Bliss found herself going on, not caring to be more or less told to shut up by anyone, 'that the lady in question realised in time that you, and your charm, were not quite what she wanted.'

Immediately the words he had drawn from her were out, Bliss wanted them back. It was his fault, of course, he with his terse cold manner was responsible, of course, for never had she known herself sound so insensitive to anyone's feelings.

She was on the brink of apologising, but was glad that she had not when, his tone cutting, his look harsh, 'The fact that Paloma Oreja, the lady in question, as you call her, and I did not get engaged—nor do I expect to see her again—is, *señorita*, none of your business!'

'As I may have remarked before, *señor*,' Bliss bridled, stung by his tone, stung by what she saw as being taken to task in a public dining-room, 'your charm is quite overwhelming.' With that she glared at him, and, as her sweet arrived, she then concentrated her attention on that.

As caramels went, her pudding was average, but it did not take long to eat. She was only halfway through it though when, realising that Quin Quintero must be hurting inside from having recently been given the 'thanks, but no thanks' treatment, she felt sorely pulled to voice an apology for her earlier insensitivity.

She was again glad that she didn't get the chance though for, after several minutes of neither of them having a thing that they wanted to say to each other, he suddenly chose that moment to break the silence.

'How about you?' he questioned coolly, his slate-grey eyes pinning hers as she looked up at him.

'Me?' she questioned, not with him at all.

'Your fingers are ringless,' he commented by way of enlightenment, 'but that doesn't mean a thing these days.'

'Oh,' Bliss caught on, something in his tone at once needling her. 'I'm not married,' she told him shortly.

'But there *is* a man in question?'

Bliss supposed since she had not hesitated to put a few prying questions herself that he should do so in return was only fair. Though, having already owned to having had no other date that evening, it seemed a matter of pride that she shouldn't let him know that she had no steady boyfriend either. Ned, she realised, had his uses. 'The man in question,' she drawled, 'is named Ned Jones, but—that's my business.' With that, she glared at him and reached for her coffee.

She had drunk nearly all of it when just then a couple of expensively turned out young men entered the dining-room. Bliss knew that they were resident in the hotel and over the last few days, as she had with a few other people, she had got into the way of nodding a greeting of some sort. She saw no reason to be churlish now just because she happened to be dining with one of their countrymen.

Both men beamed a smile her way, and she smiled back—and then had her ears assaulted for her trouble. 'It might be a good idea if you restrained your impulses to ensnare every man you meet while you're in Peru,' Quin Quintero snarled. 'You may not——'

But Bliss had had quite enough—she hadn't wanted to dine with the brute of a man anyway. 'If you've nothing else to say, *señor*,' she cut him off as she got to her feet, 'I'll bid you goodnight.'

He too was on his feet, and a look of disdain was in his expression again when, Bliss having first-hand knowledge that—given that he had just the barest trace of an accent—he was as at home in the English language as she was, he went one better than her goodnight, as, stiffly, he bade her, 'Goodbye, *señorita*.'

Bliss walked straight-backed away from him, feeling that she had never disliked any man as much as she hated him. How *could* he warn her against flirting with every man she met, how *could* he? That was what his crack about restraining her impulses to ensnare every man she met was all about, wasn't it? How dared he?

The only consoling part about it as far as she could see as she let herself into her room was that she'd left him with no illusions that she had any interest in ensnaring *him*. Though, from what had been revealed over dinner, she rather thought she'd have been wasting her time anyway. For it was clear that he was still in love with some female named Paloma Oreja.

Not, Bliss thought when some while later she undressed and got ready for bed, that she cared a button where his heart lay.

Some ten minutes later Bliss got into bed. She then put out the light and snuggled down among the covers. She didn't care a bit. She had done what she had had to do to protect her protective sister from being anxious about her and, having done that, she could now forget all about Quin Quintero and get on with enjoying more of what Lima had to offer. He could go hang. With luck, perhaps she wouldn't ever see *him* again.

CHAPTER THREE

BLISS slept well that night and got up the next morning with her energy renewed. She bathed and dressed and planned her itinerary for the day. First the gold museum, then the archaeological museum and the National Museum of History which, if she'd got her directions correct, was right next door.

Ever an early riser, she went down to breakfast early, wondering as she went if she should carry through her stated intention to her sister of going to Arequipa. She wanted to visit Arequipa before she returned to England, but there was so much else she wanted to see as well, and she'd already used up the best part of one week of her holiday.

To go to Cuzco, too, was an absolute must in her book, since Cuzco, the capital of the Inca empire, was undoubtedly most important. Should she go to Cuzco first? she pondered. Perhaps she could go to Cuzco, take in a trip to the well-preserved Inca city at Machu Picchu, return to Cuzco, and from there fly on to Arequipa.

Bliss was feeling good inside when, in a sunny humour as she considered her happy options, she entered the restaurant. Then promptly any trace of a smile that had been on her features swiftly departed. For there, virtually alone in the room, and looking straight at her, was none other than Quin Quintero.

Bother the man! she thought crossly, but carried on walking as though just seeing him sitting there halfway through his breakfast had not upset her at all.

'Good morning,' she greeted him civilly when, deciding not to invade his privacy, she halted by a table about half a dozen away from his.

'*Buenos días, señorita,*' he responded with an unsmiling but slight inclination of his head, and Bliss disliked him some more when, just before she turned from him to take her seat, she saw what she was certain was a look of relief cross his features that she had chosen to seat elsewhere than at his table.

Wretched man, she fumed; as if she wanted him to entertain her at the breakfast table! One meal with him was quite enough, thank you.

Realising that although until a few short minutes ago she had felt in quite a bright humour she was now feeling a bit down, Bliss sipped from a cup of coffee which an attentive waiter had just poured her and tried to recapture her earlier feeling of well-being.

She wouldn't let Quin Quintero upset her—why should she, for goodness' sake? He was nothing to her, absolutely nothing, so why should he upset her? Grief, she was more than happy that he clearly preferred to breakfast alone.

Her annoyance with him dipped a little when she thought of how last evening he had revealed that some woman named Paloma Oreja had turned him down. Perhaps he wanted none other than his lost Paloma to share his breakfast table, Bliss cogitated, and then stopped making excuses for him.

The man was a brute; it wasn't that he'd been thinking of his lost love when she'd decided to sit elsewhere than at his table, but that, his promise to his friend Dom kept in that he had dined with her and had asked if he could assist her in any matter, he now considered his duty done.

Bliss promptly then put Quin Quintero out of her thoughts. Though, when she had thought she might again indulge in a scrambled egg and ham breakfast she suddenly discovered that she wasn't in the least hungry.

Having finished her coffee, there was nothing for her to remain in the restaurant for. Without so much as a half-glance over her shoulder—she assumed he'd be either concentrating on his breakfast or reading his paper anyway—she got up from the table and un-hurriedly left the restaurant.

From there she went down to the hotel's enquiry desk. 'Miss Carter,' the young man in charge sur-prised her by remembering her name. 'Please, how may I help you?'

Five minutes later Bliss had decided that she would go to Cuzco the next day, but that since Erith and Dom would almost certainly insist on making the one-and-a-half-hour car journey from Jahara to meet her plane, she would not notify them of her arrival until she got there. Indeed, since it had never been her in-tention to live in Erith's pocket when she'd set out on this trip, and since she didn't want them spending their happy honeymooning days in toting her all around the Cuzco area, she might not contact them until she had completed her sightseeing.

'It will be my pleasure to ring the airline for you, if you wish,' the desk clerk assured her, as he looked soulfully into her large green eyes.

'Could you get me on the flight to Cuzco in the morning?' she was just in the act of asking when from the corner of her eye she saw Quin Quintero go,

without so much as a glance in her direction, briefcase
in hand, by the desk and out through the revolving
doors of the hotel.

Toad! she thought, not wondering any more why
that man should make her so cross. Having passed so
close, he must have seen her—she hoped the handle
came off his briefcase! One *'Buenos días'* a day was,
quite obviously, all that she was worth in his book.

Bliss forgot all about him once she passed through
the gates of the Museo 'Oro Del Peru', and wandered
from exhibit to exhibit in the gold museum, taking
her fill not only of the splendid gold of the costumes
on display, but of the necklaces and artefacts the
museum housed.

She was still within the grounds of the museum
when she had a cursory look at the several shops in
the site which sold anything from an alpaca poncho
to postcards. There was also a very small outdoor
cafeteria where she sat with a cup of tea and where
the tame deer which wandered around the grounds
came up to be fed. Since, however, there was an of-
ficial notice to be seen advising against feeding them,
Bliss fought an inner tussle where the pleading big
brown eyes of the deer were weighed against the
notice. On balance, though, the deer looked to be well
enough fed, so she decided against treating them to
a bun.

After the gold museum, Bliss visited the archaeological museum, and, having looked and admired
for some while, she discovered it was gone lunchtime.
She was feeling decidedly hungry when, having come
to a courtyard where shrubs and trees, geraniums and
oleander grew, she saw that a few yards further on

there was a café where hot meals were still being served.

Bliss wasn't quite sure what it was that she'd ordered, but the plate of rice and lima beans, and, if she wasn't mistaken, a few onions, was quite palatable. It was as she finished her meal that she suddenly realised that since this was her last day in Lima she'd better sort out what in particular she didn't want to miss.

She spent the rest of the afternoon at the Cathedral, and then went on to an art gallery, and returned to the hotel, tired but happy. She was in two minds about going down to dinner, though, and realised that she was feeling wary about bumping into *him*.

Good heavens, she scorned, why in the world should she feel wary? Within the next half-hour she had showered, donned her red dress, and was on her way to the restaurant.

She did not see Quin Quintero that night, and returned to her room trying to discover why, after such a super day, she should suddenly feel flat.

She attended to her packing, realising that she was probably more tired than she had thought, and realising too that Quin Quintero had obviously either checked out, or, since there was definitely a virile look to him, had a date that night.

Bliss went down to breakfast at her usual time the next morning, but the only *'Buenos días, señorita,'* she received came from the waiter.

'Buenos días,' she replied, and realised that Quin Quintero *had* checked out, and that she had seen the last of him.

Or so she thought. But when she had taken a taxi to the airport and had checked in her overlarge case, and, after a short wait, had walked on to the plane and taken her seat, who should come down the aisle but—Quin Quintero!

She wasn't sure that her mouth didn't fall open in her surprise. But more surprise was to follow when, there being one or two other seats vacant besides the one next to her, where should he halt in his stride, but right where she was sitting.

'Good morning,' he greeted her coolly, as he opened the overhead hatch and stowed his briefcase.

'Good morning,' she responded equally coolly, realising that the reason he wasn't showing any surprise that she should be on the same plane as him was because it was natural that she would travel about since she was here on holiday. As he took his seat next to her and strapped himself in, though, she was confused to know whether she was quite glad to be travelling with someone she knew, or whether she was not at all thrilled that she was going to have to put up with his company as far as Cuzco.

Bliss wondered if the greeting they had exchanged would be the full extent of any conversation as the plane took off, but no sooner were they airborne than Quin Quintero turned to her to civilly comment, 'Going to Jahara?'

'I—might,' she replied, with more honesty than thought, she later realised.

'Dom isn't meeting you?' Quin immediately enquired.

'Dom and my sister had decided on a three-month honeymoon,' Bliss saw she had better tell him. 'Naturally I shall call at Jahara and say "hello" before I return to England, but since I consider that they're still on their honeymoon I don't want them to think they have to show me around.'

For about two seconds, Quin looked at her long and levelly, then, having filed her comments away, he said, 'You're interested in archaeology, I believe?'

Bliss reckoned she had Dom to thank; it seemed that as well as telling his friend that she was 'sweet, gentle and with a pleasing personality' he must also have given Quin a hint of where her interests lay.

'That's right,' she replied, and thought that that was quite sufficient about her. 'Do you live near Cuzco too?' she enquired, to take the talk from her, but thinking it logical that since he and her brother-in-law were still friends it was likely that they lived in the same area. Belatedly, though, she remembered that Cuzco was situated inland—hadn't Erith said something about him living on the coast?

'No,' he replied. Bliss anticipated that there would be more but he added nothing. Nothing, that was, about where he did live or why he was flying to Cuzco, but, after a pause, he, as though refusing to be shaken off, brought the subject round to her again. 'You've been very ill recently, so Dom tells me.'

Bliss wished that Dom had not told him so much. 'I had a spot of pneumonia,' she replied, trying to make light of it, then finding that he was the type who, when he wanted to know the ins and outs of everything, wasn't so easily put off.

'I thought, what with modern-day medicines, that pneumonia was now no worse than a heavy attack of flu?' he commented, a question there in his voice, that, somehow, even if briefly, she found that she was answering.

'So it is.'

'But you had an exceedingly bad bout?'

Bliss threw him a fed-up-with-his-questions look—he didn't bat an eyelid. 'Yes,' she replied tartly.

'In both lungs, in fact.'

'Yes!' she told him irritatedly.

She could have hit him over the head with something when he pressed, 'And?'

Bliss gave him a speaking look, but then realised that it seemed he was a man who must have his curiosity satisfied. She wasn't ready yet for Erith and Dom to know that she was so near, but when she realised that if she didn't answer Quin Quintero's questions she couldn't put it past him not to ask her brother-in-law when next he spoke to him, she was anxious that he had no cause to mention her at all.

'And, since you must know,' she said heatedly, 'I had a relapse, then returned to work too soon, caught another severe chill, and was taken home from work one day.'

'And in fact, are still on sick-leave now?' he suggested.

'No—that is . . .' She broke off, realising that Dr Lawton had never actually said that he thought she was fit enough to return to work yet. 'Anyhow, I'm quite well now,' she told him with finality.

Bliss had a naturally pale, not to say translucent complexion which went superbly well with her Titian hair and had been much admired in the past. But as Quin Quintero flicked an all-assessing gaze over her features there was not, as far as she could tell, a glimmer of admiration in his look. Not that she wanted his admiration—perish the thought! She half expected, though, that he would make some terse remark on her paleness, and was consequently much relieved when he, seemingly as bored with the subject of her health as she was, chose to remark on something totally different when next he spoke.

'What work do you do?' he enquired casually.

Put out the flag, Bliss thought as she realised that there was something about her which he apparently did not know. 'I work in a library,' she saw no harm in telling him, but by then she was a little tired of being the target of his questions. It was then, though, as she was trying to think of something which would take the conversation away from herself, that a sudden thought struck her which caused her some alarm. 'You're not going to Jahara, are you?' she blurted out anxiously.

Her alarm was noted, she saw, as Quin stared into her worried green eyes.

'You truly meant it when you said you considered the newly married couple were still on their honeymoon,' he drawled.

Which to her mind, was no answer at all. 'Are you?' she insisted.

'You're a romantic,' he accused urbanely, but as Bliss stared at him, obstinately refusing to take that for an answer, a trace of a smile passed over his features and he told her, 'I've no plans to visit Jahara this trip.'

For all of two seconds Bliss felt a sense of relief. But that was before her enquiring mind started off again. Dom had telephoned Quin in Lima about her, hadn't he? Perhaps they were always ringing each other about something or other! They must be, mustn't they, for Dom to know—when he'd wanted someone trustworthy to look her up in Lima—that

Lima, where Quin did not live, was where his trustworthy friend could be found?

'How did my brother-in-law know that you were in Lima this week?' she abruptly asked, as she realised that since Quin had put up at a hotel it must mean that his visits there were of the spasmodic kind which did not necessitate him keeping an apartment. 'You must have contacted him to let him know,' she felt compelled to add when the slate-grey-eyed Peruvian merely stared back at her for her sauce.

Her large green eyes widened further, though, when he threw in, 'Intelligent as well as beautiful,' as a by-the-way before he sardonically let fall, 'Since it seems to worry you, *señorita*, you might be relieved to know that sometimes six months may pass in between phone calls.'

It was of some relief to know that, but Bliss wanted more. 'Are you saying that it could be another six months before you'll speak with each other again?'

'I shouldn't think so at all,' Quin replied coolly, to make her spirits drop. Then, making her feel faintly murderous towards him when he could have put her out of her misery five minutes ago, he added, 'Dom's building a boat for me—we'll probably be in contact in a month or so about it.' He shrugged and then went on, 'I told him I was in Lima for a few days when I rang to discuss, among other things, how the boat was progressing. The next day, shortly after your sister had phoned you, Dom rang me. The rest,' he drawled, 'you know.'

Didn't she just? Bliss mused as they lapsed into silence. It was done now, but she'd rather by far that Dom had never rung his friend. He'd done so for Erith, or course, but, whether Quin Quintero thought she was a romantic or not, Bliss thought crossly, as the plane flew nearer and nearer to Cuzco, they *were* on their honeymoon, for goodness' sake, and in her opinion this was a special time for the two, and they should not be bothered by other people.

Which thought made her doubly certain that she didn't want the 'newly married couple' as Quin put it to have to worry about anything but their two selves.

Thoughts along these lines occupied her for the remainder of the journey. So much so, in fact, that when the plane landed in Cuzco she was sorely tempted to ask Quin Quintero, should he find cause to contact her brother-in-law over the next few days, not to mention that she had been on the same flight as him, and was in fact in Cuzco.

She decided against it when, on leaving her seat, he stepped back to allow her to go in front and she looked up straight into what appeared to her to be a pair of mocking grey eyes. 'Thank you,' she murmured, and left it at that. She went down the aisle in front of him, realising that he was the type of man who would do just what he wanted to do anyway. To try to get him to understand how important she felt it to be that her beautiful and protective sister was left free to bask in her husband's love, and, for once, not think of others but only herself, and him, would, she saw, be a complete waste of time.

Bliss was aware of Quin Quintero when, in the luggage claim area, she waited for her case to arrive. He was quite some distance away from her, though— she liked it that way.

Having claimed her large suitcase, however, she was mentally practising her *Dónde puedo tomar un taxi, por favor?* which, if she'd understood her phrase book correctly, was what one said when asking any official-looking person where she might find a taxi, when suddenly her case was taken from her hand.

'That's much too heavy a case for such a slender female, *señorita*,' said a voice she was beginning to know well, as, ignoring her 'Do you mind?' expression, he, while coping with his own suitcase plus briefcase, carried on striding to the exit.

He had found a taxi without any problems by the time Bliss—who had angrily refused to run after him—had, at a fast walk, caught up with him. But her anger went up another notch when to her astonishment she saw that not only her suitcase, but his *too* was being loaded into the taxi.

'What's going on?' she demanded heatedly, as Quin looked around to observe she had made it to the taxi.

'Which hotel are you booked into?' he queried.

'I'm not,' she replied, 'yet,' and, as the taxi driver seemed anxious to be on his way, it was more from thoughts that time was money for him than anything, that she found, when Quin opened the passenger door, that she was getting in. He joined her.

No sooner were they sitting down than the taxi was off. By then, however, Bliss had got her second wind. 'Just what do you think you're doing?' she began furiously.

'From our conversation on the plane, it's clear to me that you intend to stay in a hotel while you're in Cuzco, rather than to intrude on your sister's honeymoon,' he coolly commented. 'From your reply just now of not being booked in anywhere, I feel it incumbent upon me to see to it, on your brother-in-law's behalf, that you stay in a decent hotel.'

'There's no need for you to see to anything!' she flared. 'I'm perfectly able to look after myself. I'm——'

'You've been ill!' he rapped bluntly.

Bliss, who was feeling ready to scream if she heard another word about her illness, caught sight of the driver's eyes on them through the rear-view mirror, and realised that, although he probably couldn't understand what they were saying, it must be pretty plain that they were having an argument.

'I'm better!' she hissed at Quin Quintero from between clenched teeth. 'I don't need a nanny!' she began to warm to her theme, 'Nor——'

'Good,' he cut in. 'I've no intention of being one.'

'Then for——'

'But, in view of my many years' friendship with your brother-in-law——' he ignored her as though she had never tried to get in '—and in view of the fact that whether you like it or not you *have* recently been seriously ill, I cannot abandon you to haul that suitcase around while you look for accommodation.' He had his eyes fixed fully on her when, 'You're looking very flushed as it is,' he told her; smugly, she thought.

When he stretched out a hand and touched her brow as if to assess if she had a temperature, though, Bliss suddenly wasn't thinking at all. For, at the unexpectedness of his hand on her forehead, the whole of her skin began to tingle. It took her but a moment to get herself together, and in no time, as she shrugged his hand away from her and stared determinedly, for once unseeing, out of the taxi window, she formed the opinion that if she was indeed flushed then the only reason for it was that she was growing more and more furious with this man Quin Quintero!

The taxi was pulling up outside a smart hotel by the time she had cooled sufficiently to begrudgingly be able to see that, as Erith and Dom had advised her on which hotel to use in Lima, perhaps Quin's doing the same in Cuzco was something she should accept with good grace.

Any thoughts of good grace departed rapidly, however, when, as she got out of the taxi, he got out too. She turned, nevertheless, and was still intending to do her level best to thank him kindly and wish him a civilised goodbye. To her amazement, however, she saw him pay off the taxi driver, and noted that the driver was handing not only her suitcase to the porter who had come out from the hotel—but that of her industrialist companion also!

'You're not staying here *too*?' she demanded, as he propelled her inside, somehow averse to having him around when, as her brother-in-law's good friend, he might automatically keep a weather-eye open on her.

'This hotel's big enough for both of us!' he rapped. That's what you think, she fumed silently, and looked towards the exit. She might then have followed through what seemed like a good idea and got the porter to take her case outside and stop the first cruising taxi, had not Quin Quintero breathed silkily, 'Unless of course you'd rather I rang your brother-in-law to see which hotel he would recommend for you.'

'Don't you *dare* ring him!' Bliss exploded before she could think, and was promptly on the receiving end of the arctic blast from a pair of unfriendly slate-grey eyes. Clearly, he did not take kindly to being spoken to in such a way.

Well, tough on him, she silently railed, but he had the upper hand since if she didn't want him to put a call through to Jahara she had to stay at this hotel.

Resignedly, she went over to the desk. He came and stood next to her. 'You have business to do in Cuzco?' She couldn't resist one last bite.

'That's none of your concern!' he told her cuttingly—and for the first time in her life Bliss felt the urge to hit a man.

She did not hit him, however, but nor did she have another word to say to him. She was the first to be allocated a room. Without a word to him, still smarting from being as good as told to mind her own business, she turned and, following the porter, walked away.

Once in her room, though, she sank down into a chair, and owned to feeling strangely vulnerable. Grief, she stirred herself, as she tried to shrug the feeling off, there was nothing wrong with her that a good lunch and a bit of a rest from her travels wouldn't cure.

She didn't feel particularly hungry, she realised, but since she had no intention whatsoever of succumbing to another illness—not so much as a head cold would she tolerate—she decided that in the interests of staying healthy she would put her feet up for a half-hour. After that, she would go and have a walk round Cuzco, and maybe find somewhere to eat.

Bliss returned to her hotel at a little after five that afternoon, after having spent a most agreeable time. She'd visited the city square, had lunch at the Café Roma and had wandered around some outstanding

Inca stonework, feeling glad just to be there in
Cuzco—the city shaped like a puma. More by luck
than judgement she had found herself in Hatun-
Rumiyoc Street, and in that street of Inca granite she
had looked at the high wall in particular until she had
found the famous twelve-angled stone that fitted in
so perfectly.

Once showered and changed, she decided on taking
an early dinner. She was sure, as she drank her
pumpkin soup, that her decision had nothing to do
with the fact that by so doing she would minimise the
risk of bumping into one Quin Quintero. She had a
lot she wanted to do tomorrow: an early dinner, then
back to her room to work out her itinerary before
making an early night of it seemed to her to be only
sensible.

Strangely, though, for all her good sense, she felt
it most peculiar that when her meal was finished she
should return to her room with an odd feeling that
something was missing. How extraordinary, she
puzzled, and, while she felt she could be certain that
having not seen Quin Quintero since before lunch
could have nothing to do with it, she could not help
but wonder if there was some previously unknown
perverse side of her nature that enjoyed clashing
swords with him!

By morning she was quite over the absurd notion
that not having seen Quin Quintero had anything at
all to do with her feeling that something was missing.
Grief! If anything she was probably going through a
patch of homesickness.

Which again was odd, because so far as she was
aware she hadn't thought of home or either her father
or stepmother any more or any less than anyone else

might who was on what she considered to be a trip of a lifetime.

Bliss, having not seen Quin at breakfast, forgot about him when she stepped out into the city that had been the capital of the Inca empire. She headed first for the cathedral that had been constructed in the sixteenth century on the foundations of the Inca palace of Wiracocha, and from there to the Korikancha, a convent that had been destroyed by earthquake in 1950. Thanks, however, to the architectural techniques of the Incas, the foundations had remained intact.

It was around lunchtime when Bliss, deciding to be sensible, stopped for a bite to eat and ruminated over the best way to see everything else she had on her itinerary for that day. It would take hours and hours if she walked everywhere, she realised, and, upon that realisation, the decision seemed made for her.

By way of an obliging taxi driver, and given that she had found everything of exciting interest, she did not hurry. But four hours later, having spent a pleasant afternoon taking in all that she wanted to see, Bliss, feeling sublimely happy, returned to the hotel.

Because she was tired, but no more than was normal after a full day of climbing uphill, going downhill, and generally scrambling over ruins, Bliss decided to put her feet up for a short while before dinner.

At seven she got up and showered, and then dressed in her silk trouser suit. She was in no hurry when, with her head still full of everything she had seen, she went down to dinner.

'A table for one, *señorita*?' A smiling waiter hurried forward, and led the way to a table that had two place settings.

'*Gracias,*' she smiled, and was in love with the world as she took the menu from him.

Her head was bent over the menu when another voice addressed her. 'Shall I share your table?' enquired an English-speaking, only very slightly accented voice which she knew.

Bliss looked up. Yesterday she might have considered telling him to get lost—and risked him giving her a short pithy answer which she wouldn't have liked. But that was yesterday; today she was feeling on top of the world—and she supposed it had to be a plus that the arrogant man had *actually* asked if he might share her table. 'Please,' she smiled, and at that invitation Quin Quintero took the seat opposite.

She was about to return her attention to the menu, though, when she suddenly noticed that he was staring longer than was perhaps necessary at her hair. Defensively she touched a hand to her tresses, unaware that her hair reflected in the overhead artificial light was really quite something.

'Is—something wrong?' she quickly asked, trying not to think of the possibility that perhaps she had picked up a creepy-crawly in between leaving her room and arriving at this table.

'Not at all,' he said to her utmost relief, and actually smiled the most riveting smile as he added, 'I hardly dare to ask, but is your hair naturally that most amazing colour?'

Yesterday, she would have given him a short and sharp answer for his nerve to suggest that it might have come from a bottle. Today, he had smiled—the first time she had seen a smile on him—and, she owned, the effect was pretty devastating.

So, she nodded, returned her hand to her lap, and hid her impression that he was something else again when warmth entered his eyes and that, aside from his perfect teeth, when his mouth curved in good humour it might melt the hardest heart, and told him simply, 'It is. Though don't ask me how I got it, because both my parents had dark hair.' For some unknown reason then Bliss actually experienced the long since forgotten feeling of shyness! Of wanting this quite good-looking Peruvian's attention on something else. 'Erith, my sister, has the same colour hair, so it's not unique,' she quickly told him.

She then found the menu of monumental interest, and studied it as though savouring every item, when in actual fact she was taking the time to wonder what in creation had got into her. It was strange, to say the least, that Quin Quintero should only have to smile at her and she should, if not exactly go to pieces, then have some very peculiar notions indeed enter her head.

By the time she'd told the waiter that she'd like soup, followed by something called *lomo salteado* which her experimental soul hoped wouldn't taste too foul, she had got herself together to realise that the excitement of her day had much to answer for. Most definitely she wasn't in the least shy of Quin Quintero. As for thinking he had a devastating smile—living at a higher altitude than she was used to must have affected her brain, she thought in disgust.

Her soup, when it arrived, was not the best she had tasted and she thought better than to offend her stomach by sending it down, so quietly she replaced her soup spoon and hoped for better things for the next course.

'I realise that you have an adventurous streak and prefer to make your own mistakes,' Quin suddenly murmured from across the table, 'but, had you allowed, I'd have been pleased to help you with your order.'

'That's—kind of you,' she replied politely, but could have sworn as she looked at him that he was having the hardest work to hold back a grin. She knew then that if *lomo salteado* happened to be the most awful thing she had ever tasted she was going to eat every scrap.

As it turned out *lomo salteado* proved to be morsels of beef sautéd with onions and peppers and served with fried potatoes and rice.

'It's good,' she told him, when he hadn't asked.

'I'll take your word for it,' he replied blandly, and then enquired, 'Have you done anything to satisfy your archaeological soul today?'

'You'll wish you'd never asked,' Bliss replied and all at once found that she felt completely at ease with him as, tackling her *lomo salteado* as she went, she told him of her visit to the cathedral, and to the Korikancha.

'You have had an enjoyable day,' he commented, his glance on the enthusiasm that shone like a light from her large green eyes.

'Oh, that was only this morning,' she told him. 'After lunch I went to the fortress of Sacsahuaman— did you know that some of the foundation stone blocks weigh more than a hundred tons?' she got carried away to ask in awe. 'All hauled up there from about five miles away. It must have taken thousands of men...' She halted. 'I'm sorry, you probably know the history back to front and here's me...'

'It's always interesting to hear it as seen through a fresh pair of eyes,' Quin told her, and there was such charm in him as he said it that any return of awkwardness which Bliss might have experienced was swiftly sent on its way. Though she reckoned that she had told him all of Sacsahuaman that she was going to when, 'Please go on,' he insisted.

'Well . . .' she said hesitantly, but as she thought of her day she could no more hold back than fly. 'Well, after that fortress,' she resumed, 'I, with the kind help of a taxi driver,' she inserted with a smile, 'went a few miles on to Kenko.' She forebore to tell him anything of how that Inca shrine dated back to the days of Huayna Capac, or to mention that it probably dated back further than that, but, with her eyes once more aglow, she added, 'From there I went to Tambomachay.' Tambomachay she had found very interesting; it had been a bathing area of the royal women of the Inca court, and was fed by water from a hillside spring.

Bliss was about to go on to tell him of her visit to Puca Pucara which was said to have served as a sentry post for Cuzco and the Urubamba Valley, when she began to fear that, since not everyone was interested in archaeology, she might be boring him out of his skull. Yesterday that wouldn't have bothered her.

She looked at him, and he looked pleasantly back, but when it became obvious that she had told him all that she was going to of her exploits that day he did not press her for more, but commented drily, 'It never occurred to you to save something for tomorrow?'

And suddenly Bliss's face broke out into a beautiful grin. She had thought that she hated this man, but here he was teasing her, and, she realised—as she flicked a glance down to her pudding plate to see that she had finished her meal without realising it—she didn't hate him at all.

'Tomorrow, *señor*,' she told him happily as she looked up again, 'I'm hoping to go to Machu Picchu.' With that, she stood up and was ready to return to her room.

'It will take you all day to get there and back, Bliss,' he replied and, rising to his feet too, he looked down at her. She was still getting over her surprise that he had called her by her first name when—where once she could be certain he would have been much more blunt—he commented, 'If you won't take unkindly to the suggestion, you might enjoy Machu Picchu much better for a good night's rest.'

There was a wealth of charm about him, Bliss realised, and even a hint of his former smile was in evidence. And as she stared at him she knew that had he last night—had she seen him—suggested that she had an early night, she might well have gone for his throat. But this *was* a trip of a lifetime and, even leaving aside his charm, which was something else again, she realised just then that she didn't want to fight with him.

'That sounds like a good idea,' she smiled, and was about to leave when he suggested,

'Quin.'

'Quin,' she obliged, and, as suddenly her heart started idiotically to increase its beat, she turned abruptly about and went swiftly out of the dining area.

CHAPTER FOUR

THINGS always looked different in the morning, Bliss reflected when, with a packed lunch kindly provided by the hotel in her large canvas carry-all bag, she sat in a taxi heading for Cuzco railway station. Last night—quite forgetful of what a tough customer Quin Quintero could be—she had actually believed herself happy in his company! She had even called him Quin, she recalled, and had thought him charming—now how about that for a switch?

This morning, however, she had no illusions. Quin Quintero had the ability, it seemed, to be barking and snarling one minute and putting on the charm the next. She ignored the fact that a good twenty-four hours had passed in between her walking away from him without a word on Saturday, and him coming to share her table last night, and she grew of the opinion that the next time she came up against him he would in all probability appear ready to chew her up and spit out the pieces.

Peculiarly enough, though, when this time she endeavoured to eject the man from her thoughts, she discovered that, most oddly, he refused to be ejected.

Pin your thoughts on something else, she decided, and tried to exchange the memory of slate-grey eyes which were warm with a smile that, though rarely seen, was quite sensational, for a memory of Machu Picchu. Not that she'd been there, but since a picture of Machu Picchu seemed to dominate every travel brochure that

featured Peru she could quite clearly remember what
it looked like.

She had again been grateful to helpful hotel staff
who had smoothed the way for her, for the male on
duty on the desk when she had gone to enquire about
the day's trip early that morning had seen to everything for her.

Even down to finding her an English-speaking taxi
driver, she discovered as she alighted and parted with
some of her Peruvian *intis*. 'You come here,' he told
her when she found herself in what looked like a
station yard.

Bliss had thought that she would be travelling all
the way by train, and then wondered if she had made
her enquiry so late that the train was fully booked,
for her taxi driver led the way to where a coach was
parked.

With every faith that the desk clerk back at the hotel
would have given the cab driver definite instructions,
it seemed logical to Bliss to board the coach and await
results.

She nevertheless felt to some degree better about
things, for all the adventurous spirit which Quin had
observed she possessed, when she saw that there were
other people on the coach, among them a smattering
of tourists.

She took an empty double seat by the window and
suddenly realised that the coach must be going only
part of the way, because, if memory of everything
she'd read served, there was only one way to get to
that most well-known lost Inca city, Machu Picchu,
and that was by rail.

A shifty-looking man whom she was not too thrilled
about came and sat next to her. She was not opposed

to being on the receiving end of an admiring glance now and then, but she definitely didn't care at all for the way the man made a meal of ogling her before she turned her head away.

Having realised that they must at some point be exchanging the coach for a train, Bliss was staring fixedly out of the window hoping that it would be sooner rather than later, when suddenly, she heard someone addressing the man next to her. Perhaps it was the fact that whatever the newcomer said was uttered in a tone that brooked no refusal that made Bliss think she knew that voice from somewhere.

Curiosity being what it was, she discovered that she just had to abandon her steadfast concentration out of the window. She turned her head and had the shock of her life to observe the tall and well-built dark-haired man standing in the aisle. Standing in the aisle and clearly waiting for the man next to her to move. Suddenly and idiotically her heart turned over.

'Good morning, Bliss,' Quin greeted her as the other man slid reluctantly out of his seat, and he came and occupied it.

'*Buenos días,*' Bliss smiled, and suddenly felt lighter-hearted. 'Are you going to Machu Picchu too?' she enquired.

'It suddenly struck me,' he replied easily, 'that while I've taken in quite a bit of what other countries have to offer it's quite some time since I took a look in my own back yard.'

'Machu Picchu is in your back yard?' she laughed, and saw his eyes go down to her curving mouth.

'Of course,' he replied, and then the coach driver got in, and the coach started up, and excitement began to stir again in Bliss. In a little under five hours she

would be seeing Machu Picchu for herself—she felt
most grateful that with Quin having asked the previous occupant of the seat to move she felt better able
to relax and enjoy everything.

Within half an hour of the coach setting off they
were travelling in attractive countryside where tall trees
dotted the landscape. Fifteen minutes after that and
there in the distance Bliss saw the snow-capped Andes.

'Fantastic!' she gasped and instinctively turned in
her seat, wanting to enjoy it with someone. She saw
with a slight start that Quin was watching her, not
the view, and realised that her exclamation of pleasure
must have attracted his glance to her. 'You've seen it
all before, of course,' she mumbled, feeling a little
self-conscious suddenly.

'But never on a mild day in August with a flame-
haired English woman for company,' he replied gal-
lantly, and somehow Bliss didn't feel self-conscious
any more.

She turned her head to stare at the passing scene
out of the window. Had there been an implication
there that he would keep her company for the whole
of the day? Thinking about it, thinking of how she
had instinctively wanted to share her pleasure of the
snow-capped Andes, she realised that she would quite
like his company.

For the next half-hour Bliss enjoyed the by now
totally rural scene from the coach window, while occasionally her thoughts would flit away to the man
next to her. As yet she had no idea where in Peru he
had his home, and, unless she asked her sister, she
very probably would never know. Not that that was
important, but she couldn't help wondering if the real
reason for Quin making this trip today was on ac-

count of his perhaps not wanting to go home. Perhaps his ex-girlfriend Paloma lived in the same coastal region and perhaps, with her rejection of his marriage proposal so recent, he wanted some breathing space, some time to accept her refusal before he saw her again. Though that couldn't be right, she remembered, for hadn't Quin said that he never expected to see his love Paloma again?

Which meant, of course, that wherever his lost love lived, it could not be in the vicinity of his home. Bliss then went on to wonder what then had triggered his decision to go to Machu Picchu today—or had it been his intention all along? He hadn't mentioned it at dinner last night, though, had he, when she had told him that Machu Picchu was where she was heading today? She was just into thinking that maybe, since nobody could work *all* the time, Quin must have decided to kill his spare time—and at the same time perhaps hope to lose some of his loneliness of heart—in the popular tourist spot where there were certain to be crowds of people, when a small frown puckered her otherwise smooth brow.

'Something is wrong, Bliss?' Quin suddenly asked, and she realised that he must have happened to glance at her at just at the moment when she was feeling, oddly, not very happy about his reasons to be willing to keep her company.

'I was just wondering——' she took her eyes from the clear crystal waters of a river that they were travelling alongside '—what—er—the name of that river is,' she replied, pride decreeing that she told him anything but the truth, which she hadn't sorted out for herself yet.

'It's the Urubamba,' he informed her, his eyes staying on her face for a second or two, before the coach suddenly halted when a steer appeared from nowhere and decided to cross the road in front of them.

Bliss went back to her contemplation of the view outside the window, and wondered again at the sudden appearance of perversity in her nature. She was sure she didn't give a light that she was being used as a substitute companion for the woman who held his heart—a poor substitute at that, Bliss thought, since there was barely friendship between her and Quin.

Perversity hardly covered it, she realised as she stared from the window. Why should she, who had a reputation for being choosy about her men friends, and who because of that had more friends who happened to be men than men to whom she was romantically drawn, suddenly feel decidedly—miffed? It must be a perverse sort of pride in her that she should feel put out at being used as a substitute, she realised. But she was unable to analyse why—when if anything she would have thought her reaction to the inner sufferings of a fellow human being would have been to want to help in any way she could—she should feel more personally slighted.

Bliss then decided that she had no time to go into the depths of self-analysis, and a moment later couldn't see any reason why she should bother to try. She was in Peru, for goodness' sake, she was going to enjoy every moment of it. Soon she would be back in England—every second was precious.

They were travelling through a small village when, determinedly pushing all extraneous thoughts and feelings to one side, she allowed her curiosity to stir, and asked her companion, 'Can you tell me what that long pole with what looks like a flower on the end is for?'

'It's meant to signal to anyone interested that the occupant has *chicha* for sale,' Quin replied, and, looking at him, Bliss could see nothing in his pleasant expression to give away that he must be hurting like crazy inside.

'*Chicha?*' she questioned, trying to keep her voice level when, unexpectedly, she suddenly experienced a feeling of softness for him.

'Home-made alcoholic brew,' he replied, and Bliss smiled, and turned her head to look out of the window.

She was over her moment of softness and was wondering what in creation had come over her when the coach stopped, and she realised when everyone got out that they must have come to some sort of terminus.

'Where are we?' she asked Quin as she tried to keep near him while anyone who looked like a tourist was besieged by scores of vendors trying to sell their, for the most part, highly coloured hand-crafted wares.

'Ollantaytambo—we——'

'No!' Bliss exclaimed in astonishment.

'You've heard of it?'

'It's on my list of places to visit,' she replied, her enthusiasm ever to the fore as she thought of her readings about Ollantaytambo, a town which was still lived in and whose houses and streets had been preserved exactly as the Incas had left them when fleeing the Spanish.

'There's no time now, I'm afraid,' Quin told her as if already recognising some of her eagerness from the light starting to shine in her eyes. 'We'll be catching the train to Machu Picchu shortly.'

'So I'll come tomorrow,' Bliss, in good spirits all at once, grinned. Tomorrow she promised herself, she would come again to Ollantaytambo. Tomorrow she would see the town, see the spectacular agricultural terraces she had read of, and the impressive lookout post that was said to have been built in isolation bang in the middle of a mountain. She turned and on impulse, and because she couldn't resist it, she bought a brightly coloured wall-hanging from a smiling young woman who, at the same time as serving her, was nursing a sleeping child.

'What are you going to do with that?' Quin teased as, the wall-hanging in her possession, they walked the few yards to the railway station.

In truth, Bliss wasn't quite sure. Her room at home was decorated in pastel shades and the red, yellows and purples of the wall-hanging were definitely going to 'shout' should she hang it in her bedroom.

'I'll think of something,' she laughed, and, folding it very carefully, she packed it into her canvas carry-all bag.

'That's a very big bag for such a little woman!' Quin commented.

Little! She was five feet nine in her tights-clad feet! 'I've got my lunch in it,' she told him a shade defensively.

'Ah!' he exclaimed, and Bliss just had to laugh again. It was plain from the look on his face that to bring a lunch with him was something he had not thought of.

Her good spirits stayed with her when the train with its orange- and yellow-painted coaches pulled in and he followed her into one of the compartments. The seats, in omnibus fashion, all faced the one way, and she had no objection to make when Quin chose to sit next to her.

They conversed quite easily while they waited the quite lengthy time for the train to set off. But, when at around midday their train started to pull out of the station, Quin fell silent and left her to observe what she would from the train window, as if guessing that she didn't want to miss a thing.

Half an hour or so later, Bliss noticed that the vegetation was changing. 'There are more trees here,' she glanced back at Quin to observe.

'It's the start of the rain forest,' he told her, and Bliss returned her attention to the window.

She then looked to the other side of the train where through the window she saw that the river Urubamba was bubbling white and frothy over some rocky terrain.

After its period of being tossed over the rocks, it was flowing peacefully when some ten minutes later Bliss relaxed to gently absorb everything about her.

It was uncanny, she felt, that Quin seemed to be able to read her mood exactly for it was only then that he decided to make any remark that might lead into any sort of a conversation.

'You've travelled abroad before, of course?' he queried then.

'Oh, yes,' Bliss assured him, 'but never this far.'

'You're plainly enjoying what you're seeing so far,' he commented.

'I suppose it's about time I grew more sophistication,' she remarked, up until that point having been unconsciously quite comfortable with the person she was. Quin, now, he was sophisticated. So, too, she'd like to bet, was Paloma Oreja.

Bliss was just beginning to find how contradictory she was in that she was certain that she didn't want to be like any Paloma Oreja, when to her surprise, not to say pleasure, Quin, after glancing at her face which was almost free of powder and paint, remarked easily, 'Part of your charm, Bliss, is the way you are just you.'

'Is it?' she questioned, a shade warily, she had to own, not certain that there wasn't an intended sting in there somewhere.

'Believe it,' he said, and seemed sincere, and then smiled that quite devastating smile, and Bliss suddenly found something of very great interest outside.

It was about one-thirty when he left his seat and came back carrying a parcel of sandwiches and a couple of containers of liquid refreshment, and Bliss just had to smile. He might not have thought to bring a packed lunch but it was unthinkable that the gods would allow him to starve. He handed her one of the containers of liquid, and it seemed as good a time as any in which to dive into her bag to see what sustenance the hotel had prepared for her.

It was the first time she'd had a picnic on a train—she enjoyed it. 'I'll go and take a look at the hand-washing facilities,' she told Quin when she'd finished, and as he stood up to let her go by and her shoulder brushed his chest she realised that this close he was indeed tall and that perhaps she did seem 'little' to him.

She was glad to have stretched her legs but as she retook her seat she discovered that there was not much longer to go now. The train went first through one tunnel, and then through another and at exactly ten past two the train pulled into Machu Picchu station.

Excitement started to soar in Bliss. She was here, actually here in Machu Picchu, the city that until 1911—apart from local villagers knowing of its existence—had been lost to the outside world.

She could have, and would, she supposed, have managed quite well on her own. But it was so much nicer being with someone who had been there before. Because Machu Picchu was somewhere high up in the mountains, it appeared, there was only one way— unless, if you were superhumanly fit, walking it—to get there.

She was being besieged by a fresh lot of vendors, when Quin said, 'This way,' and took charge of her elbow. She was happy to go with him and they were soon with a mass of other travellers all queuing up for the small twenty-four-seater mini-coaches that would take them up and ever up the hair-raising zig-zagging path to the mountain city that sat high in the midst of other mountains.

It was a thrill a minute after that. Bliss hung on tightly as the minibus made its tortuous way upwards. Their destination reached, Quin stepped off the coach first at the end of their ride and turned to help her alight.

'Are you all right?' he asked as, taking her hand in a firm grip, he held on to her as she stepped down and turned her so he could see into her face.

Her heart was racing, from the excitement of it all, she knew. But she didn't want him remembering, now of all times, that her brother-in-law had mentioned that she had been ill. There was much to see, and she wanted to see it all before, as needs must, they had to go back down the mountain and catch the train.

'Never better!' she told him stoutly.

He continued to survey her steadily for a few more moments, but, when he seemed ready to believe her, she felt she could be magnanimous and let him carry her bag when, taking it from her, he enquired, 'What would you like to see first?'

'Everything,' she laughed—and he laughed too, and all was right with her world.

The ruins of Machu Picchu were situated high up between the two peaks of Machu Picchu—which in Quechua, one of the languages spoken in Peru, meant Old Mountain—and Huayna Picchu, which meant Young Mountain. It was the tall peak of Huayna Picchu that was most often seen in pictures of the site. The ruins had been discovered by an American senator and professor, and for the next two hours Bliss had a wonderful time walking, admiring, climbing and clambering over Dr Bingham's discovery.

Those two hours were never going to be sufficient to gaze and wonder at the agricultural terraces, the industrial section, the temples, the houses, the fountains built like steps, all of which rose two thousand feet up from the Urubamba valley.

Once, she missed her footing, but Quin was swiftly there to catch her by the arm. 'Steady,' he said quietly, and as she looked up at him, serious grey eyes looked down into hers. She had a feeling that her cheeks might be slightly flushed from her exertions, and, because she was feeling a little out of breath just then, she had no argument to make when, as if he was aware of the pressure her recently inflamed lungs were under, he kept a grip on her arm and she was forced to rest for a few minutes.

'Is that the road we travelled on in that bus?' she asked him, staring in awe at the thirteen-hairpin-curved road in the near distance that snaked back and forth up the mountain side—a modern-day construction compared with the ruins which surrounded them.

'Looking forward to going down?' he teased, an indication there, she felt, that the ride down was going to be even more of a white-knuckle experience than the ride coming up.

With so much to see it was not surprising, as visitors to the ruins went off in all directions, that when they reached the ruins of a control tower Bliss should find that she and Quin were alone.

She was feasting her eyes on the granite block of the tower, however, when suddenly she was caught by an attack of coughing which, no matter how hard she tried, she could not gain control over. She flicked her glance to Quin, and away again—he had been looking intently at her.

'Is that the Urubamba—river flowing—right down there?' she tried to take his attention off herself by pointing way down to the bottom of the mountain where a river could be made out winding its way. Her attempt to take Quin's attention from her proved useless when what she was saying was interspersed with her coughing.

'Don't talk,' he instructed her calmly, and, taking a few steps closer to her, he suggested, 'Try to relax.' To her surprise he came yet closer and gave her the benefit of his manly chest to lean on.

Gradually, her coughing eased, though it took some minutes before she dared think it was definitely over, for, just when she was thinking that it was done, she would start off again.

'I'm—sorry,' she said at last, but when she would have pulled back from him, she discovered that his arms had come about her in a loose hold.

'Rest for a few minutes,' he quietly instructed the top of her head, and suddenly, as she leant her weight against him and his strength, a kind of peace seemed to wash over her—somehow she hadn't realised how tired she was.

But, while she found that there was a certain— pleasure seemed to be the only word that would fit— in being held secure in his arms, Bliss was recovering more and more all the time.

She remembered how Erith had told her that high altitude was no respecter of persons and latched on to that to excuse her coughing bout. 'It must be the altitude,' she told him as she pulled back. She then looked up and anything else she might have found to say went out of her head completely. For as she looked into Quin's eyes she saw that he, looking down at her, seemed to be suddenly shaken somehow. She felt his arms that were still about her tighten—as if without his knowledge. She looked down and focused her attention on one of his shirt buttons, feeling oddly in need of getting herself more together. Then abruptly Quin's arms about her were relaxing their hold, then his hands had come to her arms and he was quietly, but firmly, putting her away from him.

His hands were still on her arms though, his tone even and showing that the thin mountain air must be playing tricks with her imagination too, and that he was not shaken about anything when he decreed, 'Then I suggest, Bliss, that we'd better see about catching our train.'

Since there were a good few places where it was impossible to walk two abreast, it was Quin who led the way back to the bus terminus, his pace even, un-hurried and giving her no chance to get breathless as she walked slowly behind him.

He was rather thoughtful, quiet, she felt as they got on a bus, and she wondered as it set off if perhaps he was a little fed up with her company.

That thought occupied her completely for about a quarter of the way down and then she, along with Quin and all the other passengers on the bus, became aware of the tracksuit-clad Peruvian boy who ap-peared from nowhere and attracted their attention by giving a mighty yell. At first Bliss had no idea what was going on but as the bus slowed prior to nego-tiating every bend of the hairpin road, so the boy of about ten or twelve would, with the same mighty yell, wave his arms in the air to attract their attention.

'He's racing us!' Bliss forgot that Quin might be fed up with her to turn to him to exclaim.

'You may be right,' he agreed, and there was such a pleasant look on his face for her, that, with her heart leaping inside her, she just knew that if he was quiet it was not because he was so fed up with her after all.

Bliss felt she really liked him very much indeed when she saw the young boy, who was wringing with per-spiration, having run all the way down the hillside to be there to meet them as they got off the bus, ac-cepting a substantial note from Quin's wallet.

The rail station at Machu Picchu was alive with tourists, an army of traders, and much noise and bustle. The whole area was colourful with children, stray dogs, sights and sounds and Bliss enjoyed it all as Quin, with his hand on her elbow, took her with him through to the railway waiting-room where it seemed to her that traders had been banned. There was a refreshment area in the waiting-room, though, and she was glad when, after leaving her for a few minutes, Quin returned with some orange juice and a couple of rolls.

'Thanks,' she smiled, and was glad of the drink and, since they had some hours of travelling to do yet, thought perhaps it might be a good idea if she had a bite to eat too.

At a little after five-thirty the train pulled out of the station, and as Bliss settled down to the journey, she realised that she was exceedingly tired. From experience she knew that a bout of coughing could take the stuffing out of her—but that had been when she'd been ill, she argued.

Rats, I'm fine, she thought in disgust, and decided that a prolonged coughing bout, at high altitude, would be tiring even to the fittest.

Quin was quiet again, she mused, and again she had the uncomfortable feeling that he was fed up with her. He'd been pleasant, though, she thought drowsily, forcing her eyelids apart when they wanted to close. Perhaps it was just that he was generally fed up, the thought nagged. He was heart-sore over Paloma Oreja, that was for sure.

Bliss tried to eject both Quin and his ex-love Paloma from her mind. Somehow she didn't want to think about them. She didn't feel comfortable with them in her head. It annoyed her somehow to think of Quin and his love.

Her thoughts for no reason had just flitted on to remembering how Quin had held her in his arms up at Machu Picchu, when her eyes started to close again. It had been kind of him to let her rest against him until that exhausting bout was over, she thought. Very kind...

Bliss stirred, stretched out a hand, and touched something solid. 'Have a nice sleep?' enquired a gentle voice somewhere by her ear, and abruptly she woke up.

'Oh, I'm sorry!' she apologised, and on becoming aware that she had her head on Quin's shoulder she rocketed to sit up straight.

'Any time,' he drawled, but there was such a relaxed way about him that suddenly Bliss just had to smile. 'You were done in,' he excused her pleasantly, and asked, 'How are you feeling now?'

For answer Bliss consulted her watch—it read ten to eight. 'Have I been asleep for two hours?' she questioned, appalled that with her head on his shoulder for two hours he must have felt pinned to his seat.

'You know, of course, that you snore?'

'I don't!'

'True, you don't,' he replied, and Bliss realised she loved his teasing. She looked out of the carriage window and saw that they seemed to be speeding through a main village street. It was then that she realised that, as well as loving Quin's teasing, she also loved his country. Peru had woven a spell about her and, like her sister before her, she had fallen in love with Peru.

She had thought that they might have to disembark at Ollantaytambo and go from there by coach, as they had in reverse on the outward journey. But it was just around nine o'clock, after some shunting backwards and forwards as if for impetus to climb a steep gradient, that they arrived in Cuzco.

With the train emptying its cargo of passengers, Bliss was glad that she was with Quin, a man who knew his way about. For in no time he had secured for them a taxi, and they were on the way to their hotel.

Bliss stood with him at the reception desk as they waited for their room keys. Then, the keys to hand, she went with him to the lifts. 'No need to ask if you've enjoyed your day,' he commented as they waited for a lift to arrive.

'Machu Picchu's something else again,' she smiled, and got into the lift with him and as he pressed the lift button to the floor they were both on, she suddenly, in the closed confines of the lift, was taken by the most ridiculous shyness.

As she was wondering what the dickens was the matter with her—she'd left shyness behind years ago, for goodness' sake—well, save for being tripped up by it fairly recently—the lift doors opened.

She got out of the lift, fully expecting that in the larger space of the corridors to the rooms on that floor any ridiculous feeling of shyness would disappear. But not a bit of it, for as Quin halted for a moment with her before going on to his room, and looked down at her to suggest, 'Shall I see you in the dining-room in fifteen minutes?' she just couldn't get the words out to agree.

'I'm—not hungry,' she told him and, without staying to wish him goodnight, which she considered was ill-mannered in the extreme, she walked quickly away from him, and to her room.

Half an hour later she climbed into her bed accepting that while it was true that she didn't feel in the least hungry it would have been quite pleasant to spend half an hour or so with him in the dining-room. She *could* have eaten something, little though that something might have been.

She put out the light, deciding that another early night would top up on her reserves of strength so as to ensure she would be ready for Ollantaytambo tomorrow.

Strangely though, when on every evening since she had been in Peru she had always gone to sleep with what she would do the following day to the forefront of her mind, she went to sleep that night with her thoughts quite elsewhere.

Machu Picchu was marvellous. Quin had been a very pleasant companion and, all in all, she rather thought that today had been one of the best days of her life.

CHAPTER FIVE

BLISS slept soundly that night but, most peculiarly, she awakened the next morning and still felt tired. She was later than usual in getting out of bed, and found that she was having to push herself to get ready to start the day.

She tried, as she got bathed and dressed, to pin her thoughts on her intended visit to the Inca town of Ollantaytambo but to her bewilderment she discovered that her keenness for the visit had gone completely!

Bliss made her way down to breakfast still wondering where the dickens the enthusiasm with which yesterday she had viewed the trip she had planned to make had gone to. She entered the hotel's restaurant and saw at once that Quin, his breakfast over, was finishing off with a cup of coffee.

A few days ago she would have ignored him and gone and sat elsewhere. Today, she had grown from disliking him intensely to liking him quite well. She made her way over to his table, but he had seen her and was already on his feet by the time she reached him.

'Buenos días,' she greeted him, and, as he had once, she asked, 'Shall I share your table?'

His answer was to pull out a chair for her. But she was shortly to wish that she had left him to finish his breakfast by himself. For he very soon noticed that apart from fruit juice and coffee nothing else passed her lips, and he seemed to see no reason why he should not comment on it.

'You're not hungry this morning?' he questioned.

Bliss shook her head. 'It's not unusual,' she replied, and cosily thought that that was the end of the subject. But no, Quin Quintero, his expression stern, was there with another question.

'This habit, of occasionally not wanting breakfast, is a recent one,' he pressed.

'Recent?' she queried, not with him at all. Grief, some people ate heartily at breakfast, others didn't!

'Since your illness,' he clarified.

'Oh—really!' Bliss exclaimed huffily, not wanting to be harangued by him or anyone else. 'Lots of people never eat breakfast,' she told him shortly. 'To some people, the thought of eating anything at all before noon is positively alien. In any case——'

'But I've seen you eat, and enjoy, a plate of scrambled eggs and ham at a very early hour,' he cut her off, and Bliss glared at him. Trust him, while probably not even taking any notice of her, to absently file away what a waiter had carried past him, for further use if need be.

'Well, today I'm just not hungry,' she told him defiantly, and as without comment he just sat and scrutinised her face, and because yesterday she had quite liked him, and because she suddenly discovered that she didn't want to be bad friends with him, she found she was excusing, 'I'm very often not hungry when I've had a big meal the night before.'

'But you had no meal last night,' he reminded her sharply, and while Bliss wanted to give herself a nip to wake herself up—too late now to remember how she had not been hungry last night either—she just then decided that she'd had quite enough of this interrogation.

She was not liking Quin Quintero one little bit when she began, 'Look here——' only to get sliced off before she had so much as got started.

'What sort of a night did you have?' he bluntly cut in.

'If you must know, I had a very good night!' she told him belligerently. But cursed the pure femininity in her that meant that when he just sat looking at her, she had to ask, albeit as though she had no interest in his answer, 'I look a wreck?'

Slate grey eyes that had already done a thorough study, she had thought, roved over her clear brow and unblemished complexion. 'You look beautiful, and you know it,' he answered to her surprise, though the grittiness of his tone took away any idea she might have that he'd intended his remark to be a compliment.

'Then I must have slept well,' she told him coolly, and, having decided that that was quite enough about her, she took a quick last sip of her coffee, and made to gather up her things. 'I'm a little later than I meant to be this morning,' she told him, trying to keep her tone conversational. And, forcing enthusiasm where she felt none, 'I must go to the desk and see what arrangements I can make for visiting Ollantaytambo.' She had her belongings neatly together when, as she glanced at Quin prior to wishing him a polite goodbye, she saw him move his head from side to side. 'What are you shaking your head for?' she enquired; a trace tartly, she had to own.

'You've done quite enough chasing around looking at things archaeological,' he told her coolly. 'Today,' he decreed, 'you will rest.'

Witlessly, disbelievingly, Bliss stared at him. For stunned moments she couldn't believe that she had heard what she had just heard. 'What?' she questioned incredulously, while her brain tried to absorb that this man, this man, this friend of her brother-in-law, had actually said what he had. Had actually had the nerve to think that he could tell her, no order her, decide for her, what she could and could not do!

To her further amazement, he looked in no way abashed for having been asked to repeat what he had said. But, ignoring the fact that she was staring at him as though still trying to credit her hearing, he announced, 'Look at you, all big-eyed and white-faced. I don't suppose——'

'I've always been big-eyed and pale!' Bliss cut him off before he could get started. The sauce of the man! Who in creation did he think he was that he should tell her, 'Today, you will rest'? 'I've always——' *He* cut her off this time.

'. . . been stubborn,' he supplied.

'Not at all!' she snapped. 'I read a lot about Peru before I came, and have so many places I want to see before I——'

'How long have you been here now?' he annoyingly cut her off again to query.

'Er—nine, no, ten days,' Bliss worked it out, and even then wasn't sure that she'd calculated it right. But that was beside the point. The point was——

'And how many of those ten days have you rested?' Quin Quintero, not content in cutting through her words, cut through her thoughts to question.

Grief—as if she had time to rest with there being so much to see. She could rest when she got back to England, for goodness' sake. 'There's no time,' Bliss tried to get through to him. 'It's——'

'Bearing in mind that four months ago you were critically ill and fighting for your life,' Quin again interrupted her flow, causing Bliss to realise that by the sound of it her brother-in-law had given him a pretty thorough run-down on her, the woman he'd asked Quin to see if he could do anything to ease things for, 'do you think it's wise not to take a break?'

'Look, Quin,' Bliss tried another tack. While on the one hand she wondered what in blazes she was doing still sitting there arguing the case when to her mind there was no case to argue, memory of the kind way he had let her lean against him yesterday when she'd had a coughing fit tempered her crossness that they were having this conversation at all. 'Look,' she said again, 'I've about another ten full days left before I head back to Lima to catch a plane back to England, and I still haven't done, seen, half the things I must see before I go.' Quin was looking steadily at her as she itemised, 'I must get to Trujillo in the north and visit Huacas del Sol and de la Luna, and I've promised myself I really must take in the white city of Arequipa in the south, while at the same time it's unthinkable to me that I return to England without taking a look first at the lines of Nazca, which I think is somewhere in between the two.'

'You seem to have a very full programme, Bliss,' Quin, his glance still steady on her, remarked easily.

Bliss smiled; she thought she could afford to. She hadn't mentioned that she still had to find time to pay a visit to Erith and Dom at Jahara before she flew back to England too. But with Quin seeming to understand that she couldn't afford to let up for a moment if she was to complete her schedule she was glad that she had stayed to explain how things were rather than just walked off—as she had felt like doing.

She owned, to herself but no one else, that she felt rather drained—doing battle with him hadn't helped—but she smiled on as, magnanimous in victory, she quietly told him, 'So you see, Quin, I really don't have time to put my feet up before I go home.'

He smiled too, and she was quite liking him when, 'And you're absolutely set on going to Ollantaytambo today?'

Bliss liked his smile also, and, for all her enthusiasm had still not returned, she ignored the fact that, in truth, she didn't feel much like tackling the upward climb which she'd read was involved once she'd got to Ollantaytambo. There was no way in which she was going to say otherwise now.

'Absolutely,' she replied, and added pleasantly, 'I'm looking forward to it.'

For several long seconds Quin just looked at her, and his expression was as pleasant as hers when, leaning back in his chair, 'That's a bit of a pity,' he casually drawled.

'A pity?' she questioned, tilting her head a little to one side. 'I don't think I understand.'

'Then permit me to allow you to understand,' he returned, and there was that in his voice, all at once, that suddenly made her wary. 'You are insisting on visiting Ollantaytambo. I, *señorita*, insist that you do not.'

'You insist . . .?' Bliss started to erupt, and, having not missed that she was all at once *'señorita'* again, she was suddenly as furious with herself as she had speedily grown with him. When she took a sharp intake of breath, though, a particle of dust, air, or some other agent hit the back of her throat, and she was forced to break off to cough.

Fortunately, her coughing bout was short and nothing at all like the paroxysm that had taken her at Machu Picchu yesterday. But it was all Quin Quintero needed to hear; with no sign of a smile about him then—just a toughness which she had no liking for—he stated, 'And, by the sound of it, I am right to insist.'

'You have no rights over me whatsoever!' she hissed, outraged. 'How dare——?'

'While you're in this country you're under your brother-in-law's guardianship. Your br——'

'I've never heard anything so——'

'Your brother-in-law has passed that guardianship over to me, and——'

'Now, just a minute!' Bliss, aware that there were other tail-enders at breakfast, was having the hardest work in the world keeping her voice down.

But Quin Quintero, her newly appointed and most definitely unwanted guardian, was not giving her so much as a minute. Instead, his tone every bit as aggressive as hers, he was losing no time in telling her bluntly, 'You're not one hundred per cent fit. Anyone with half an eye can see that. But, since it seems that you—wilfully and stubbornly—refuse to take my advice and rest——' advice, was it? Funny how it came out sounding like a no-argument-about-it-bossy order '—then you leave me with only one course of action.'

Do your worst, Bliss wanted to fire back, but, knowing him, she didn't doubt that he would. 'And what might that be?' she tilted her chin to ask belligerently.

'What else,' he shrugged, 'but contact my old friend, and acquaint him with the fact that——'

'That's coercion!' Bliss exclaimed angrily. The swine, the diabolical... Words failed her as she fumed at how Quin Quintero, knowing full well by now that she'd do anything rather than upset her sister's honeymoon, seemed all set to contact Jahara to tell them *his* opinion that she wasn't well.

'So?' he enquired blandly, having been watching her and apparently not a bit put out by the changing expressions of fury on her face.

You swine! Bliss silently fumed, and grew so angry then that she was ready to try to bluff. 'So,' she shrugged, inwardly boiling, 'I should care.'

'You're saying that you don't?' He didn't look convinced, and again Bliss shrugged.

'Since I'd planned to call in and see Erith and my brother-in-law any day now, I can just as easily go tomorrow,' she told Quin loftily, then saw that he was studying her as though deciding on something.

Bliss was feeling wary again, but to her surprise Quin did not call her bluff, but told her, that pleasant tone back in his voice again, 'I'm afraid, Bliss, that you'll have a long way to go if you intend calling on the newlyweds.'

She looked at him sharply. He seemed sure of himself—and she didn't like that. 'You know something I don't?' she questioned uneasily.

She saw one arrogant eyebrow raise aloft, then again he shrugged and, looking completely unconcerned, said, 'Unless you rang Jahara, as I did last night, you won't know that very early this morning Dom, and your sister, left Peru, for—France.'

'France!' Bliss exclaimed in total astonishment. 'They've left... But they'd cut short their tour because Jahara called to them so! They'd come home to Jahara for the remainder of their honeymoon because...' She broke off as she suddenly thought of Dom's tall and elegant French mother who'd crossed the Channel from her home in France to Ash Barton to see her son married. 'Is Dom's mother ill?' she questioned urgently, that being the obvious reason, in her view, why Erith and Dom would leave Jahara in such a rush. And they must have left in a rush, Bliss considered, or Erith would have been bound to have mentioned her plans to visit France when they'd spoken on the phone less than a week ago.

'You've met Madame de Zarmoza?' Quin queried in return, his face expressionless as, ignoring the fact that she had asked if Dom's mother was ill, he waited to hear if she had met her.

'She came to Erith and Dom's wedding,' Bliss replied, realising that since he had called Dom's mother by the French *'madame'* she preferred to the Peruvian *señora* Quin *must* have met her too. 'Didn't Erith want to speak to me when you rang last night?' Bliss suddenly thought to ask. 'I presume you told Dom that I was staying in the same hotel?'

'I didn't speak with your sister,' Quin replied evenly. 'When I told Dom, however, that you'd had a busy day and had retired early, he seemed to think it best not to disturb you.'

Bliss tossed Quin a cross look and was about to flare that she'd be glad if he'd keep out of her affairs. Though she could see, with everything happening so quickly, that Erith would have enough to do packing for her flight to France. 'You told Dom I was all right, though?' she questioned in sudden panic. Erith had sufficient to think about without worrying over her. 'You didn't tell them about that silly coughing bout yesterday?' she swiftly tacked on, knowing that Erith would for certain worry about it if he had.

Bliss, her gaze urgent as she waited for Quin to answer, saw the thoughtful look that came to his face. And she did not like it at all when—perhaps seeing her anxiety for his answer, he did reply. 'Not—then,' he drawled, and there was that in his tone which she considered most threatening.

'What do you mean—not then?' she bit, the breakfast-room temporarily empty of guests save for the two of them, but that no longer bothering her, so incensed was Quin Quintero starting to make her.

'Are you still *insisting* on visiting Ollantaytambo today?' he replied silkily, and Bliss no longer silently thought him a swine.

'You swine!' she hissed. 'You...' More names of the same uncomplimentary nature might have followed, but just then Bliss's brain patterns started to wake up and, riled and rattled, she wasn't choosing her words when she told him shortly, 'Do your worst, Quintero.'

For long moments he said nothing but sat and stared at the angry sparks flashing from her large green eyes. 'You're trying to tell me something?' he softly enquired then, his gaze never leaving her face.

Bliss smiled, a sweet and phoney smile, before, 'You, *señor*,' she told him, and there was almost a purr in her voice, 'have just said goodbye to any blackmailing hold you had over me.'

At the least, she thought, he might show a touch of chagrin, but no, he did not so much as flicker an eyelid. 'Forgive me, *señorita*——' he too smiled, a smile which this time she did not like at all '—but this time it is I who don't understand,' he replied pleasantly.

Not much, you don't, Bliss fumed, and took the greatest satisfaction, in drawling, 'Then permit me to allow you to understand.' Her tone had undergone a sharp change, though, when she added bluntly, 'With Erith and Dom no longer in Peru, you'd be wasting your time ringing Jahara to tell them anything that would cause my sister to be alarmed.'

She leaned back in her chair. In a minute she would gather up her things again and see about getting to Ollantaytambo. But, just for a minute, she felt she had earned the right to an unladylike gloat.

Quin Quintero allowed her ten seconds of that minute, then, that silky note back in his voice again, he asked pleasantly, 'You think I don't have their phone number in France?' His drawl beat hers into a cocked hat.

Swine was too good a name for him, Bliss fumed, as first she wondered if he really had Madame de Zarmoza's number in France, and then realised that if he hadn't—since in all probability he also knew Dom's sister Marguerite, not to mention Marguerite's son Filipo, Madame de Zarmoza's grandson—there were countless ways in which he could find out, even if they had flown to France too.

'You wouldn't ring, though, would you?' she questioned at long last, her triumph short-lived as she started to taste the ashes of defeat.

He didn't say *'Try me,'* but it was all there in his lofty look. Bliss was hating him, and wondering what the devil she'd ever done to have him appoint himself her health's guardian when, 'Look at it this way, Bliss,' he said quietly, his tone more conciliatory than it had been. 'I've promised your brother-in-law that I'd keep an eye on you, see to it that you——'

'I don't need anyone to keep an eye on me!' Bliss interrupted hotly—and was ignored for her trouble.

'What sort of a friend would I be if, the moment he's out of the country, when you, for all your protestations to the contrary, look as though a couple of days tucked up in bed wouldn't come amiss, I left you high and dry in Cuzco and went on to Paracas?'

To Bliss's mind just then, to be left high and dry would be all that a woman could wish for. But, oddly, when she opened her mouth to get in there and tell him exactly that, to her tremendous surprise, she discovered her inbuilt curiosity had a will of its own, and heard herself ask instead, 'Paracas?'

'It's on the coast. It's where I live,' he replied, and while, with strangely mixed feelings, Bliss took on board the fact that by the sound of it he was intending to shortly return to his home in this place Paracas, he was going on to quietly astound her by continuing, 'Dom reminded me last night that you are not as strong as you think you are, and that it isn't at all advisable that you should rush around archaeological sites the whole time—the way you have been doing.'

'Really?' Bliss tried to get in, but was again ignored.

'Wasn't that how you became ill in the first place? By neglecting yourself when out in all winds and weathers you caught cold. However, with Dom sharing his wife's concern that you may overdo things, I've proposed that I take you with me to Paracas where you can relax and recoup your——'

'I'm not coming to Paracas with you!' burst from Bliss angrily before he could finish.

'I promise you you'll like it there,' Quin overlooked her ungraciousness to tell her mildly.

'No I won't—because I'm not going!' she said hotly, and was back to wanting to physically lash out at him when, after studying her for a couple of unnerving seconds, he obliquely reminded her of the alternative.

'You don't think that Dom and Erith have enough to worry about at this present time?'

'That's unfair!' Bliss burst out, but her anger was cooling as, frustratedly, she felt herself losing ground. 'Why do I have to go to—to Paracas?' she questioned. 'I could give you my word—maybe—that I won't rush around so much. I could . . .' She broke off and was on the point of changing her mind from placatingly telling him what she could do to opposingly tell him what *he* could do—when Quin, the possessor of more charm than in her opinion any one man should have, chose that moment to use it.

'Of course,' he suddenly smiled, a quite charming smile, 'if you were exceptionally good, and rather than deprive your archaeological soul entirely, I'd happily arrange for you to take a flight over the Nazca lines.'

He could not, had he known it, have said anything more guaranteed to sidetrack her interest. The Nazca lines were mysterious large lines and drawings on the stone desert floor between Palpa, Nazca and Porona.

The lines had been traced by an ancient and unknown people some four or five thousand years previously and the best way of viewing them was said to be by flying low over them in a light aircraft.

'I . . .' Bliss began, and could already feel a buzz of excitement at the thought of doing just that. She then stopped short. She didn't want to go to Paracas—did she? 'Is Nazca near to where you live, then?' she prevaricated, and felt confused suddenly because while she was certain that she didn't want to go and stay in Quin's home she suddenly felt another buzz of excitement at the very thought.

'It's nearer Paracas than Cuzco,' he answered, and for all the world as though the matter was settled, 'If you'll excuse me, Bliss, I'll go and arrange our flight as far as Pisco.' While she stared wordlessly at him—in shock, she rather thought—he got up from the table and said easily, 'If you'd like to pack your case while I'm gone, we might be in Paracas in time for lunch.'

'I'm not . . .' Bliss began, but she was talking to the air—he was already striding from the restaurant.

For five minutes more she stayed exactly where she was—rebelling. She wasn't going to any Paracas, she'd be blessed if she would. Why should she, anyway? Why . . .? Her thoughts, along with her rebellion, ceased when that 'why' brought forth the name 'Erith'. She loved her sister dearly, and had been at pains not to intrude on her honeymoon. But the fact that Dom's mother's unfortunately falling ill had caused Erith and Dom to leave Jahara in a hurry to go to her was bad enough—so was it really fair, when Erith and her new husband had enough trauma to cope with just now, that Erith, who had watched over Bliss like a hawk when she'd been ill, should have

Quin Quintero ring her in France to give an exaggerated account of that coughing bout yesterday—and of her pallor today?

You'd think he'd have more sensitivity than to think of ringing Erith at a time like this, Bliss fumed as, mutiny back with her again, she left the restaurant. But, since he'd seemed so adamant, and since she dared not push it lest he did put that call through to France, she couldn't see what else she could do but go with the wretched man.

Railing against him, Bliss went not to the desk to make an enquiry about getting to Ollantaytambo, but in an opposite direction up to her room. Once there she dragged out her case and packed her belongings. Having to remind herself again and again, whenever she paused to wonder what on earth she was doing, exactly why she was giving in to Quin 'you look as though a couple of days tucked up in bed wouldn't come amiss' Quintero.

Damn him and his promise to her brother-in-law that, because she'd been ill, he'd keep an eye on her, she fumed impotently, blackmailed into doing something that was not in her schedule. There was Nazca, of course, tempted a small voice, but she ignored it and, getting out her address book for no other reason than that sheer obstinacy declared she shouldn't accept Quin Quintero's bossy edicts without trying to find a way out, she rang her sister's number at Jahara.

'Señora de Zarmoza, *por favor*,' she requested of the voice the other end. But any faint hope that Quin Quintero had got it wrong and that her sister had not left Jahara for France yet had to be abandoned when her brother-in-law's housekeeper, she presumed, instead of going away and bringing Erith to the phone, gave forth a whole volley of Spanish. Which Bliss, while not understanding a word of it, felt she could be certain was an explanation of where her sister was at the moment. *'Gracias,'* was all she could think of to say when the good soul at the other end paused for breath.

'Gracias,' the woman replied, and Bliss heard the phone quietly go down.

And that, she sighed, seemed to be that. Bliss returned the phone in her hand to its cradle and thought perhaps it was just as well that Erith had already left anyway. It was for certain that she wouldn't have wanted to have worried her by telling her to call her bloodhound off. So, apart from assuring Erith that she was fine and to hope that she found her mother-in-law improved when she reached France, Bliss belatedly realised that there had been little point in making the call anyway.

Dear Erith, she thought, but in remembering how her sister had assured her Dom wouldn't ask just anybody to check if she was all right, and how Dom trusted Quin implicitly, Bliss wished that Dom's highly esteemed friend didn't take his promise to keep his eye on her so literally.

So I'll go to Paracas, she thought sourly, resignedly, but as for taking to her bed for a couple of days, as Quin had indicated, that most definitely was out. She was in the middle of mentally retiming her schedule and thinking that she might yet be able to fit everything in, when a knock sounded on her door. She went to answer it.

Quin Quintero stood there, tall, well-built and, in any other circumstances, rather dishy, Bliss had to admit. He had his suitcase down by his feet and his briefcase in his hand when, looking directly into her green eyes, 'Ready?' he enquired.

Bliss was anything but a sore loser, but this was one instance where she found it exceedingly difficult to 'Play up! play up! and play the game!' She swallowed hard, 'We're going now?' she asked. He nodded, and, without another word, she turned back inside her room for her case.

It was he though who carried her case from her room and to the lift. He who carried it from the lift and he—to her annoyance—who, when she halted by the desk saying that she had to settle her bill first, told her that he had already settled her account when he'd settled his.

'You can pay me back later,' he commented, when she reached inside her bag for her purse—clearly a man who wanted to be on his way.

'Love to!' she replied shortly. My stars, how she'd love to pay the blackmailing swine back!

Quin Quintero was most courteous as they went to Cuzco airport by taxi, and once there boarded what she realised was a privately chartered plane to take them to Pisco. Only when they were seated and waiting to take off, though, did she admit to feeling tired again. She looked out of the plane window while they waited for instructions from the control tower, and while she kicked against having been forced by Quin to go with him when she wanted to be the one in sole charge of her life she just then realised that, if she was truthful, she wouldn't mind a day in which to recharge her batteries. Not that she was ever going to admit that—to *him*!

It did not take very long for the plane to reach Pisco, and Bliss, who was already starting to realise that Quin must be quite wealthy to have chartered the plane, saw more quiet evidence that he was not without means when he escorted her over to a long, sleek limousine which he had obviously had parked at the airport awaiting his return.

Bliss looked around her as Quin drove from the airfield area and left Pisco behind. Soon they were in Paracas and she at once saw the marked difference in that sea and sand coastal region from inland Cuzco.

She guessed that they were on the outskirts of Paracas when Quin turned his car in at a pair of huge iron gates, and drove past an avenue of palm trees, to pull up outside a vast one-storey building.

Immediately he stopped the car, the stout wood of the double doors opened and a manservant hurried out. Quin left the car and after some brief conversation with the man went and opened up the boot.

The manservant was carrying their suitcases into the house when Quin came round to the passenger door, and opened it. Bliss did the only thing left to her—reluctantly, she got out.

'I hope you'll enjoy being my guest,' Quin told her formally. She gave him a speaking look—she wouldn't be staying that long.

CHAPTER SIX

IT WAS Friday, and the sun was shining as Bliss stirred
in her bed. She sat up and, gazing round the elegantly
furnished room that had been hers since Tuesday, she
suddenly realised, with something of a shock, that
she had been in Quin's home for three days now!

Bliss got out of bed and pattered to the adjoining
bathroom. She hadn't thought to still be here. Indeed,
she would have dug her heels in most firmly had Quin
Quintero so much as breathed a suggestion that she
should stay longer than for more than an overnight
stop.

There was no denying, of course, that she had been
more tired than she had realised. Not that Quin, with
his comments to the effect that she might benefit from
resting in bed for a couple of days, would ever have
her admitting that. Only now, as she showered and
dressed and felt so totally revitalised, did she admit
to herself that a break from charging around from
museum to museum, from site to site had been called
for.

The strange thing was, she mused as she brushed
and then combed her shining Titian hair, that,
although since an early age she had always read, par-
ticipated in, and slept and dreamt on her hobby of
archaeology, over the last three days, thoughts archaeological had barely impinged. There was a reason
for that, though, of course, she reflected. That reason

being that there was so much here at Quin's home to absorb.

It was a large home by any standards and by that Friday Bliss was acquainted with some of the people who helped to run it. There was Señora Gomez, a short, plump lady, who was Quin's housekeeper. The manservant who had carried in their cases on Wednesday was her husband Stancio who generally helped out, and a pretty young woman of about nineteen whose name was Leya, and with whom Bliss had most contact since it seemed that Leya had been assigned to personally look after her.

Bliss, clad in a straight-skirted dress of pale green, left her bedroom and went along the corridor, and down another corridor. Then she turned right into a hallway where she knew by then that she would find the breakfast-room.

She was, she realised, a little later that morning than usual, but Quin was still at breakfast when she went in. He glanced up, and she smiled, and suddenly knew that any anger she had felt against him for his black-mailing tactics had totally disappeared.

'Good morning,' she bade him pleasantly as she slipped into what was by now her accustomed seat. At that moment Señora Gomez arrived with fresh coffee and toast and Bliss answered her greeting with a cheerful *'Buenos días'* of her own. As the *señora* left the room Bliss poured herself a cup of coffee, and it was then that she became aware that Quin's eyes were on her.

She was not mistaken, she found on looking up and across at him. Her large-green-eyed gaze met his full on, but he did not look away on being caught openly studying her, but remarked easily, 'There's no need to ask how you are this morning, Bliss.'

A trace of a smile curved her mouth, as for once she felt no annoyance with him that he had clearly been looking at her so as to assess for himself the state of her health.

'No need at all,' she replied, and added happily, 'As you can see, I'm bursting with good health.'

Taking her eyes from him, she extracted a slice of toast from the toast rack, and had just placed a pat of butter on to the side of her plate, when the most cringe-making thought suddenly popped into her head.

'Naturally, I shall leave today!' she looked up quickly to tell Quin on the instant it dawned on her that, having done his duty to his friend Dom by keeping an eye on her when she'd looked in need of a rest, Quin, now that she had got her second wind, was hinting that he'd housed her for long enough.

She was about to thank him formally for his hospitality, however, when she saw his expression change from one of being startled by what she had just said, to one of amazement. 'What brought that on?' he enquired lightly.

'You—I . . .' she struggled, and then, getting herself together, told him frankly, 'I only ever intended to stay a short time, I——'

'You consider three nights under my roof a long time?' he queried, his amused look fading, his expression growing stern.

Most peculiarly, then, Bliss discovered that she didn't want him looking sternly at her. Somehow, just then, she wanted him back to being light-hearted with her.

'It's not that,' she told him, 'But, since the only reason you brought me here is because you—er—thought I needed a rest, I feel I would be outstaying my welcome if I . . .'

She broke off when Quin butted in softly, 'What a sensitive creature you are.' Bliss just stared at him. 'Am I to take it that you do not mind as much as you did that I brought you to my home?'

'I . . .' Bliss began, and wasn't quite sure what to say. Her fury, her rebelliousness against him and his method of getting his own way, had gone, that was for certain. 'Who could not enjoy being in such a lovely place?' she eventually answered with the truth that one would have to be a person totally without soul not to enjoy not only Quin's home, but its situation; it was fronted by trees of eucalyptus, palm and pine, and was backed by the sea—the Pacific Ocean.

'Are you saying that you'd like to stay with me a little while longer?' he suddenly asked, and as Bliss looked at him she had the craziest notion that the idea pleased him.

She glanced away from him, realising that even though his command of English was first-class what he actually meant was not 'stay with me' but 'stay in my home' a little while longer.

'I'm here in your country to—as well as call in on my sister, of course—see for myself some of the wonders of your archaeology, which up until now I've only read about,' she reminded him.

'Which is why, now that you're fully rested,' he inserted, 'I propose to drive you to the Museo de Sitio Julio C. Tello, this very morning.'

In an instant her gaze was fully on him. 'There's an archaeological museum near here?' she questioned.

'Quite close,' he replied, 'though it's only a very small one. But since I've decided that you have done enough tearing around trying to get to see everything at once, a small museum will be quite large enough to start you off with again.'

Three days ago, Bliss knew that she would have gone for his main artery at that '*I've* decided that you . . .' but that was three days ago. This morning her anger with him had so far faded as to have disappeared completely. He needn't, after all, so much as even consider driving, purely for her benefit, to the museum he had spoken of.

'You're not going to work today?' she queried, remembering how yesterday, and the day before, after instructing her to rest, he'd left his home to drive to his factory where he had an office, some thirty minutes or so drive away.

'You'd have me working the whole time?' he queried, and suddenly his devastating smile came out, while her heart suddenly seemed to turn a complete cartwheel inside her so that she had a hard time in keeping her own face expressionless. 'I do, as it happens, have one or two business phone calls to make,' he told her, and announced, 'We'll leave for the museum in about an hour.'

Bliss returned to her room after breakfast to find that Leya had already been to her room and that the bed she had left open to air was now made, the carpet vacuumed, everywhere dusted, and that her room was once more immaculate.

Strangely, for all she was of course interested in going to the museum, it was not thoughts of the museum and what she might see that occupied her just then. In her mind's eye she again saw Quin and that quite overwhelming smile of his. But when she searched to discover why her heart should somersault the way that it had, she could find no logical answer, no matter how hard she tried.

The Museo de Sitio was, as Quin had said, small, but Bliss spent a fascinated half-hour wandering around the totally engrossing artefacts of wood, pottery and textile which had only this century been excavated in Paracas.

It had not taken them long to reach the museum, for all it appeared to be in isolation miles from anywhere. But, because of its small size, half an hour was sufficient, Bliss found, and she had no demur to make when Quin suggested they return to his home.

'My housekeeper tells me you take a swim in the pool each afternoon,' Quin commented as he turned his car into the drive of his home.

'I sort of got the idea that I mustn't swim in the sea,' Bliss murmured, recalling how with a stream of Spanish, but more comprehensively by gesticulation, Señora Gomez had headed her off yesterday when she'd thought, while clad in her swimsuit and towelling robe, to investigate the water down by the boathouse.

'I might take a dip myself this afternoon, if you'd care to try it,' he offered casually.

'Thanks,' she replied equally casually, her tone noncommittal as parting from him to go to her room, she felt the strangest excitement grip her.

What on earth was the matter with her, for goodness' sake? she wondered, when, in her bathroom washing her hands, she caught sight of her slightly flushed cheeks in the mirror over the washbasin.

After thirty minutes of self-analysis—during which she realised that, where once it had been things of the past that could stir her to excitement, now it seemed her excitement, the fluttering in her heart region, seemed bound up not with her hobby, but with matters concerning Quin Quintero—Bliss took another ten minutes out.

She wasn't—getting infatuated by him, was she? she wondered in alarm—and found the very idea scary! Having never been infatuated with anyone before, she had no guide-lines, but she felt so unnerved by the very idea that she wanted to be certain that the whole notion was totally ridiculous.

When later she left her room she had become firmly convinced that having *physically* recovered from a surfeit of 'site'-seeing she must be *mentally* all over the place.

'You're quite well, Bliss?' Quin asked her abruptly, when, with various meats, salads and vegetables laid out in serving dishes for them to help themselves, he seemed to notice that she helped herself only to small amounts.

'I'm fine,' she told him, and really was. 'But—as you once remarked—I'm only little.' A smile broke from her, she couldn't help it. 'Besides,' she added, 'I might go swimming later.'

She saw his glance flick to her mouth, and then back up to her laughing green eyes. He said nothing more on the subject of her small lunchtime appetite, however, but helped himself to some salad, and enquired into her views about the museum they had visited.

Two hours after her light lunch, Bliss, with a white towelling robe over her swimsuit, left her room. Today she ignored the attractions of the swimming pool, and walked along the path between the wide flower-edged lawns towards the ocean.

The sea stretched out as far as the horizon, and soon she was leaving the path and the green lawns behind, and was walking on sand. She had yesterday taken a walk within the grounds of Quin's home, and today, now seeming as good a time as any in which to shed her sandals, she made for the wooden structure which she knew to be a kind of open-fronted sea-facing summer-house.

She was in the summer house looking out to the Pacific, and hoping that Quin hadn't meant that she had to wait for him before she dipped a toe in, when suddenly she heard a sound that alerted her to the fact that she had company.

'So this is why you didn't answer my knock on your door!' Quin remarked easily as he rounded the summer-house, stepped from the sand, and joined her on the ceramic tiled floor.

Absurdly, Bliss suddenly felt shy again. Grief, she thought, instantly denying any such ridiculous notion. Quin was dressed in trousers and a sports shirt, and had a towel flung carelessly over one shoulder. Somehow, though, when only moments before she had found the summer-house quite roomy, just having the height and build of Quin with her in its confines seemed to swamp her.

'The sea calls,' she told him lightly, and took a couple of unhurried paces, which brought her in a line with him. Crazily, just the fact of standing so close to him caused her heart to begin pumping energetically inside her. Then, while the sensible side of her realised that just the fact of his nearness could have absolutely nothing to do with the way her heart was misbehaving, she forced herself to walk on.

She had the sand beneath her feet when Quin fell into step with her, but she felt better away from the close confines of the summer-house. Untying her towelling robe as she went, she discarded her robe on dry sand, and walked to the water's edge.

She was an average swimmer, but enjoyed the sport, and was practising a few overarm strokes when, smoothly and without apparent effort, Quin swam by.

He went out deeper than she did, but even so, on the few times she glanced to see where he was, she discovered that he had turned back to glance her way—for all the world as though he was checking— to see where she was.

Bliss, having thought she'd got over her anger with him and his 'keeping an eye on her' penchant, suddenly discovered that she felt quite cross. She was not an invalid to be watched all the time, and Quin was not, despite what he'd said, her guardian. She was a woman, and he was a man, and... Suddenly Bliss discovered that she was utterly confused. 'Oh, hell,' she muttered, and in the next moment, as if to get away from thoughts she did not want, realisations she did not need, she was swimming like fury as if to outrace a truth that was fast catching up with her.

The outcome, which she would have foreseen had she been thinking at all clearly, was that she was out of her depth when she ran out of physical steam. She halted, took in water, coughed and spluttered and then, when it looked as though she might go under, she suddenly found herself supported by a pair of strong masculine arms.

A few seconds later Bliss came to an awareness that those strong masculine arms were now securely around her, and that she was clinging on to Quin as if there were no tomorrow! She was still somewhat confused when she grew conscious that he was treading water for the two of them. But all at once then, she started to grow more conscious—of the feel of his thighs against her thighs. Of his broad naked chest. Of the dark wet hair on it. Of their two bodies so closely pressed together. And suddenly, when she had not been aware of panicking before, she felt panic assault her. In that panic, however, she suddenly, and inexplicably started to feel that she wanted to be even closer to him. Suddenly in there too was the oddest notion, that Quin felt—the same way!

In the next second she had her hands against his naked chest and, while she kicked out instinctively with her feet, she pushed at him. And Quin, as if seeing her panic, if not aware of the cause for it, abruptly let her go.

Bliss swam back to the shore, her emotions steadying as she began to be certain she had never been going to sink anyway, and that—just as certainly—she was never going swimming in the sea in future.

Quin did not join her when she picked up her robe and draped it round her shoulders, and she was glad about that. She went back up the long path to the house without looking round.

Once she had showered and washed her hair she began to regain more of her equilibrium, but she was nowhere near ready then to examine why Quin had the ability to disturb her so. Or why, when up until then he had not given the smallest indication that he might be physically aware of her, she should have been so powerfully physically aware of him!

Leya brought a pot of tea and some daintily cut sandwiches to her room about five o'clock, but though she was glad of the tea Bliss was not hungry. Nor was she hungry when the hands of her watch showed that dinner would be served in half an hour.

She was tremendously pulled then not to leave her room, but the thought a few minutes later that with Quin taking his attention to her welfare so seriously he might well come knocking at her door saw her hurriedly changing into a dress suitable for dinner. The last thing she reckoned she needed was to have Quin probing to find out what was the matter with her if she wasn't hungry. How could she tell him something which she felt too confused to know herself?

Quin was already in the dining-room when, a minute or so after her usual time, she joined him. She realised that she was still feeling shaken when she had to take a deep breath before she opened the door. She saw his eyes on her as she went in, and was glad to have something to which pin her glance when her eyes strayed to the drinks tray. Quin had been mixing a Pisco Sour, she observed: a cocktail made from the local white grape brandy, egg white, lemon juice and a hint of sugar, which she'd sampled last night at dinner and had declared delicious.

'You've recovered from your exertions of this afternoon?' he enquired blandly, as he poured her a glass of Pisco Sour and handed it to her.

'Quite, thank you,' she replied stiffly. Was he being funny?

They had moved towards the table when the most appalling thought struck: maybe he'd seen how disturbed she'd been when she'd clung to him in the water. Oh Lord, was he now under the impression that she fancied him?

She had not been feeling very communicative before. At that horrendous thought, Bliss could not think of a thing to say. Nor could she find any appetite to eat, even though—since Señora Gomez had gone to a lot of trouble—she did her best to down some soup, meat and vegetables.

'Your appetite has disappeared again!' Quin remarked sharply when, the first and second course over, Señora Gomez had just departed after bringing in the final course.

'I can't help that!' Bliss retorted, the worst mealtime she had ever sat through in her life almost at an end. She saw him frown darkly at her, and knew that— while it was all right for him to be sharp—her sharp tone had not gone down with him at all well.

'Why can't you help it?' he challenged abruptly.

'Because I can't. I'm physically well, I assure you!' she told him irritably.

'I'm pleased to hear it!' he rapped. But he would not let the matter drop. 'So,' he went on, 'since in the head you're alert and intelligent, I . . .' he broke off and looked thoughtful for a few moments, before finishing ' . . . I can only assume that something has happened to upset you.' As Bliss had expected, it didn't take him long to pinpoint what. Though his tone was far gentler than it had been when, indicating with his head to the direction of the ocean, 'You're still shaken from thinking you were going to drown out there this afternoon?' he suggested.

'I never thought for a minute that I was going to drown!' Bliss denied hotly, with more honesty than thought, and could have groaned out loud that, when he had just handed her a perfect excuse to cover that she was so emotionally mixed up about him, she was so disorientated that she had just thrown it away.

'Ah!' he exclaimed, and was soon sharing with her what that 'Ah!' had been all about when, clearly remembering her panic, he deduced, 'But it's got something to do with your fear while I held you up out there.' Then abruptly, as something hit him, something which he patently did not care for, a shaken kind of exclamation in his own language rent the air, before he told her coldly and stiffly, 'I assure you, *señorita*, that my sole intention when I caught hold of you was to assist you. You were never,' he clipped, 'under threat of being raped.'

Bliss was not sure that her jaw did not fall open. She had not even thought of such a thing! But, having already thrown away one ready-made alibi to cover how confused she was about just about everything just then, she had no intention of throwing away another.

Not that she could allow him to believe she had thought anything so dreadful about him. But she could at least try and take his attention from her—and, since her lack of appetite seemed to concern his guardian soul, kill two birds with the one comment.

'In that case,' she replied at last, and forcing herself to weather his cold, stern-eyed stare, 'may I have a piece of that delicious-looking cheesecake?'

Bliss went to bed that night conscious that 'things' weren't right between her and Quin, but not knowing what she could do to make things right.

She arose the next morning and knew that the time had come for her to leave. She had slept poorly, and, though she was physically in top form again, she felt most decidedly out of sorts. Would Quin give her the stern-eyed treatment today should she tell him she was leaving? she wondered. She doubted it.

She made her way to the breakfast-room determined to be bright and cheerful, just as she was determined to tell Quin, with due thanks, of course, that she must leave. 'Good morning,' she smiled sunnily when she entered the room and saw that he was already there downing coffee.

She saw him place down his cup, then stare steadily and solemnly at her. Then, just as she was searching for just the right words to tell him she would shortly be off, '*Buenos días*, Bliss,' he said courteously, and then he smiled that smile, and added, 'Today, in the interests of getting you slowly back into archaeological circulation, I thought we'd drive to Ica.' And Bliss, her determination suddenly flying out of the window, was lost on two counts.

'Ica?' she queried, her interest taken as her heart gave one of its little somersaults at his smile.

'I could go on at length,' he replied, 'but I'll settle for telling you that while Paracas belongs to the province of Pisco they are both situated in the department of Ica, which is about an hour away on the Pan-American highway. If you promise to eat your dinner tonight,' he went on to tease, 'then I'll promise to show you around the Museo Regional de Ica.'

'I'll eat every scrap,' she promised with a laugh, and was so happy that—given the 'plus' of his teasing—not one stern look had he thrown her way, that she was seated beside him in his car on the Pan-American highway before she remembered that she had been determined to leave today.

I'll leave tomorrow, she decided on that instant, and gave herself up to enjoying the fertile valley of Ica, that for hundreds of years had been famed for its wines and pre-Columbian culture.

She and Quin were in the archaeological museum, and Bliss was intent on studying the ceramics and textiles on display, when she suddenly realised that she was not as totally absorbed as, up until now, she had always been. Strangely, she was conscious of Quin, standing near her the whole time.

'What did you think of it?' he asked as they left.

'Terrific,' she told him with a smile, and wondered perhaps if, unthinkably, an excess of museums had perhaps dulled her appetite.

They had lunch in a smart hotel in Ica, and Bliss felt quite relaxed as they talked easily on any matter that came up. Quin asked her about the rest of her family in England, and having told him about her father, stepmother and stepsister, Bliss then felt he couldn't mind if she asked him a similar kind of question.

'Do you have any brothers or sisters?' she questioned.

'Two brothers,' he replied unhesitatingly. 'Both married, and with sons, which...' Abruptly, then, he broke off, and Bliss was suddenly wishing with all she had that she had not asked her question. Because, plainly he had been about to state that since he could not marry Paloma Oreja he had no wish to marry anyone else. And, because his brothers through their sons had continued the family name, he could now feel free to remain a bachelor.

Suddenly Bliss felt that the very air she was breathing was filled with strain and tension. Quin was hurting inside about his lost love, she knew that, and all at once she started to feel a great dislike for the unknown woman. She also began to feel Quin's hurt—as though it were her own.

The drive back to Paracas was uneventful and silent. Bliss knew that Quin was deeply busy with his own unhappy thoughts in which there was no place for her.

She was not hungry at dinner, but, while she made herself eat something, she observed that Quin himself had very little to eat. She went to bed that night in a very sombre frame of mind.

By morning, Bliss was certain that she would be leaving that day. She arose early, and, even though it was Sunday, a day when most people forgot about putting in an appearance at their place of work, she somehow had a feeling, maybe because Quin was his own boss, that, Sunday or Monday, it made no difference to him if there was work to be done. Suddenly she felt convinced that Quin was bound to leave for his office shortly after breakfast. She had no time to consider that perhaps her thinking was a little agitated when she hastily showered, donned shirt and trousers, and wasted no further time in heading for the breakfast-room.

It was important to her that she saw Quin before he left. Good manners alone dictated that she give him her thanks personally. She went into the breakfast-room knowing that not only was her decision to leave the right one, but knowing also that, having housed her for the best part of a week now, Quin must be wanting his house back to himself, and would be looking to hear her say that she was off.

Which, when her pride alone congratulated her on her correct decision, made it a nonsense to her that she should suddenly feel a pang because after this morning she would never see him again. Ridiculous, said her head, as she opened her mouth. 'Good morning,' she smiled to Quin who put down the paper he had been reading.

'You slept well, Bliss?' he enquired, his eyes on hers.

'Splendidly,' she replied, taking her seat while at the same time noting that he was dressed not in business clothes but in a casual shirt and trousers. 'In fact, I feel so well now,' her pride forced her on, 'so full of energy, that I'm ready for anything. Which is why——' She got ready to start on her 'thank you very much' speech—only Quin chose that moment to cut in.

'Good!' he looked across the table to her. Then he promptly sent every word of her speech from her head when he said, 'Since you are now fit, do you perhaps fancy a trip to Nazca?'

'Nazca!' Bliss exclaimed—did she ever! 'I thought you'd forgotten!' she went on excitedly.

'Would I?' he drawled, his glance on the animation in her face, his look friendly.

'Are you sure?' she felt she should ask, 'I don't want to keep you from your work.'

He did not, as she thought he might, remind her that this was Sunday. But after a moment when, his eyes steady on her, he just looked at her, he then quietly replied, 'I'm sure,' and advised her, 'We'll leave at ten.'

Bliss had no idea how far away Nazca was, but none of her excitement had left her when at five to ten she met up with Quin and went out with him to his car.

'Got your camera?' he enquired.

'Fully loaded, and with spares,' she beamed.

She had been fully convinced though that they would be driving all the way to Nazca, when to her surprise, Quin swung the car into the airfield at Pisco.

'We're flying direct over the Nazca lines from here?' she queried, trying hard to hold down her feeling of excitement.

'We'll fly from here as far as Nazca—I've arranged for a commercial company to take us over the lines,' he informed her affably.

Parking his car, Quin then went to consult with one of the officials and then came back to her. Then, to her immense surprise, he took her over to where a small private plane was stationed.

'Does the pilot know we're here?' she took it upon herself to question when, without waiting, Quin opened up the plane and turned, looking ready to help her aboard.

'You're talking to him,' he grinned, and as Bliss coped with that surprise and realised that he must have booked someone else to fly them over the Nazca lines so as not to take revenue out of someone else's pocket, Quin assisted her into her seat, and instructed her to fasten her seatbelt.

It was thrill after thrill that morning, she discovered, when, with Quin at the controls, they took off. Ash Barton was going to seem very dull in comparison when she got home, she rather thought. Though, not wanting to think of returning to England, not yet anyway, Bliss put such thoughts behind her and gave herself up to the pure pleasure of the here and now.

No sooner had they taken off, it seemed, than they were landing. Quin was there to help her alight and, as she straightened up, Bliss found her glance caught and held by him. 'Ready?' he queried softly.

'Oh, yes,' she replied, and knew that the sole reason for her heart drumming so energetically was because of what she was there to see.

Without another word, Quin led her over to where a small four-seater aircraft stood. In seconds the pilot was there in conversation with Quin—and very soon she and Quin were strapped in behind him. Then the pilot started up the plane, and they were speeding down the short runway. Then, they were off the ground.

And so, for Bliss, began what was a flight of a lifetime. The Nazca lines had been first mentioned in modern times in 1927 when they were discovered by Toribio Mexia Xesspe. Since then they had been studied by many people. Dr Maria Reiche in particular had spent years and years investigating them. Many theories had been put forward into how, all those centuries ago, they had been drawn, but as far as Bliss was aware no definite theory had been agreed upon.

But she was not interested in theories just then as the light aircraft reached the lines and she looked out on to the light grey and dark grey of the desert floor to the etched lines she had up until then only read about.

'There's the condor!' she exclaimed to Quin, too busy with her camera to look at him as the pilot flew low and pitched the plane sideways so she could get a better shot, and she photographed the large outline.

For the next half-hour the pilot manoeuvred the plane over the many miles of desert and turned his plane sideways this way and sideways that for her, while Bliss—making a mental note to go back for her stomach later—did her photographic best.

It was thanks to his flying skills that she reckoned she'd got some fantastic pictures. She was sure she had a beauty of the spider—that was said to be fifty yards long—and the lizard, the whale and the monkey.

Her excitement just about peaked, though, when she saw the humming-bird, quickly shot several photographs and, without knowing it, while tipped over to the left, she stretched out a hand to the right—and had it caught—and held.

They had left the desert, and were coming in to land when, facing the front again, Bliss suddenly realised that she had a firm but masculine hand in her grip. Immediately, as she let go her hold, her glance shot to Quin.

'I'm sorry!' she apologised straight away, totally unaware that her eyes were still shining from what she had just been allowed to see.

'Don't mention it,' he said softly, his eyes fixed to hers, and then, he smiled—and it was all too much. She looked away.

On leaving the small plane, she shook hands with the pilot and thanked him very much. But she was still very much on a high when, having exchanged one plane for another, Quin took off for Pisco.

They had landed in Pisco, though, and had walked over to his car when, as he unlocked the passenger door for her, Quin looked down into her face, and with a hint of a smile there, enquired, 'Come down to earth yet?'

'Did you ever experience anything so incredibly marvellous?' she asked in reply. Then suddenly, as wordlessly Quin just stood and looked down at her—

she felt that she could barely breathe. She knew that she just wasn't breathing when, as if drawn to her by some unseen magnet, his head came nearer. And Bliss, her lips parted on a wisp of a gasp, felt Quin's mouth over hers as, gently, he kissed her.

At the feel of his warm, wonderful mouth over hers, she felt as though her heart had stopped beating entirely. Then that kiss was ended, and Quin was pulling back from her.

Bliss didn't know where she was when he turned swiftly from her. 'No need to ask if you enjoyed Nazca,' he remarked, his voice calm and quite pleasant as he went on, as if fully aware of how the flight had affected her stomach, 'If your insides are back to being your own, how about lunching in Pisco?'

Bliss laughed lightly. 'Love to,' she replied as she got into his car, but she had little thought in her head for lunch as Quin pulled away from the airfield. She thought his kiss, his gentle, giving kiss, the most beautiful thing she had ever known.

The thrill of Nazca was light years away, and she had by no stretch of the imagination got herself back together again when Quin pulled up outside a restaurant.

She supposed she must have eaten something that lunchtime, but had no idea at all what. She owned then that the effect Quin was having on her was something else again.

After their meal he drove them back to his home, but did not go in with her. His tone, though, was even when he informed her, 'I've some business commitments which will keep me tied up for the rest of the day,' and then added, his expression pleasant, 'I'll leave you to dream of Nazca.' With that he was gone.

Bliss spent a quiet afternoon. Then she showered and washed her hair. Then, although she thought she'd received a fair hint that Quin would not be in to dinner that evening, she nevertheless dressed with more care than was usual.

Quin was not in to dinner. But by then Bliss was quite happy to dine alone. For she had quite a lot to think about. Quin's beautiful and gentle kiss on her mouth at lunchtime had wreaked a quiet sort of havoc in her ever since.

She returned to her room after dinner and, deep in thought, she sank down into one of the well-padded bedroom chairs which the large room housed. She had faced by that time that fact which stubbornness and unwillingness to believe had kept at bay.

Here was the reason why her interest in archaeology had taken a back seat. Here was the reason why she was so emotionally mixed up about Quin. Here was the culprit—even her lack of appetite could be traced back to that culprit.

It had been staring her in the face for days, she realised. She had been alarmed to think that she might be infatuated with Quin. But she could hide no longer from the truth that what she felt for Quin Quintero was no mere infatuation. The knowledge of the depth of her feelings for him would be held back no longer. She, it was plain—painfully plain—was head over heels in love with him.

Painfully—because much good would loving Quin do her. For he, the man she loved, was in love with another woman. He was in love with Paloma Oreja!

CHAPTER SEVEN

Bliss slept very little that night, and as a direct consequence she was still catching up on missed sleep at a time when she was normally getting showered and dressed. When, fifteen minutes later, she did awaken and become aware of the time, she was in no hurry to start her day.

She pushed back the covers and sat on the side of the bed, wanting with all her heart to rush to see Quin before he left for his office, but the knowledge of her love for him was still new, and she hadn't sorted out yet how she should act.

Her pride decreed, of course, that she should leave his home at once, for she would never be able to live with herself should he ever guess at the depths of her feelings for him. Yet love, she was fast discovering, had a nasty way of side-stepping pride's path. For although yesterday she had been fully determined to leave Quin's home, it seemed that love, a love he must never know about, would not allow her to leave— until she had to.

Which, she realised as she left her bed, hunted up fresh underwear and headed for the bathroom, made her one very mixed-up person. For here she was, longing to see Quin again—so much so that she was putting all thoughts of leaving his home to the back of her mind—while at the same time she was dawdling to get showered and dressed, in the hope that he'd have gone to his place of work by the time she left her room.

Quin *had* gone to his office by the time Bliss reached the breakfast-room. And, just to show how contrary love could make one, she didn't know just how she was going to get through the many hours until dinner—the most likely time when she might see him again.

'*Buenos días, señorita.*' Señora Gomez came bustling into the breakfast-room with coffee and toast, seeming to have some magic antenna for when she was up and about.

'*Buenos días. Gracias, señora,*' Bliss replied, and was tempted to enquire if her master had gone to his office, but somehow managed to hold that temptation down.

For one thing it was doubtful that she would have been able to make herself understood to the housekeeper. For another she didn't want anyone at all to have the smallest inkling of how, within the last twenty-four hours, she had become aware that life, for her, began and ended with Quin.

Her appetite had not improved but because there was no way that she was going to start fainting about the place through lack of nourishment Bliss munched her way through a slice of toast and marmalade, her thoughts bleak. If the hours until dinner-time seemed endless, then how was she going to cope when, back in England, all chance of seeing Quin had gone?

When her thoughts got too much for her, Bliss left the breakfast-room. But only to return to her room to find that the fleet-footed and energetic Leya had been to her room and had been busily employed.

With nothing to do, not even a need to smooth a duster over any surface, Bliss collected a paperback, and went aimlessly out again.

Two hours later she was seated in the summer-house on the sand. She had her paperback on her lap, but she was not reading, she was staring out to sea.

She was still in more or less the same position, and still had her eyes on the water, when about an hour later she nearly jumped six inches when Quin suddenly stepped round the side of the summer-house.

'Oh!' she exclaimed, and cursed whoever had invented blushing when, as her heart leapt, she was sure her face had gone crimson.

To her gratitude, though, Quin had chosen at that moment to cast his eyes in the direction in which hers had been staring. 'You're a bit off course if you think you're looking out to England,' he commented, and turned back to stare down at her. 'Homesick for the boyfriend?' he grunted.

Bliss felt she could ignore his remark about 'the boyfriend' as she realised that, caught unawares, she must have appeared as glum as she felt. She could, of course, in her new-found love, be being over-sensitive where Quin was concerned, but it seemed to her then that good form, if nothing else, meant that she, as his guest, could not admit to feeling homesick. Which then placed her in something of a dilemma. For, while she was most definitely not homesick, she felt she could hardly tell him so in case he questioned her on why then had she been staring so dolefully out to sea.

Bliss did the only thing possible—she didn't answer his question at all. 'I thought you'd gone to your office,' she changed the subject entirely to comment, and felt her heart start to misbehave again when Quin decided to come and join her on the bench seat.

'Good book?' he queried, taking her copy of *The Pre-Hispanic Cultures of Peru*, which she'd picked up at one of the museums she'd visited, from her lap. 'Are you always this serious?' he wanted to know.

'What's wrong with serious?' she asked, but suddenly, as laughter started to bubble somewhere inside her, she felt certain that he was teasing her.

'Poor Ned Jones,' he remarked, to her astonishment remembering Ned's name.

'Why poor Ned?' she questioned, and wondered if she'd got it wrong about Quin teasing her, for suddenly his easy manner had fallen away and he was wearing such a stern expression—it was almost hostile.

'You're saying that your relationship with him is that of lovers?' he questioned sharply, and, while Bliss was at once wondering how the dickens they had got on to this subject, she felt any sign of laughter strangled at birth.

'I'm not saying anything of the kind!' she flared suddenly. 'Ned and I are friends, good friends,' she qualified, regardless that Ned might want things a little different, 'but that's all we are!'

'You're saying that he's not *that* kind of a man friend?' Quin questioned sceptically, and suddenly, while loving him, while pining for a sight of him, Bliss felt she could cheerfully have stamped on his foot.

She took a long and steadying breath, and, while she was determined all at once that Quin could go run for an answer, the fact that he was silently, harshly studying her made her reply—if only to remove his attention the quicker from herself.

'No, he's not *that* kind of a man friend!' she flared, and, since he seemed to want specifics, 'I don't sleep with him, I never have slept with him, nor do I now, or at any future date, have any plans, whatsoever, *to* sleep with him!' she underlined hotly.

There, she thought crossly, do what you will with that! She was totally astonished when he did.

'You're no longer a virgin, of course?' he questioned tautly.

'Why of course?' she retorted, rattled, wondering what the devil he thought it had to do with him, while at the same time she was still trying to glean how in creation they had got on to this subject.

'You're meaning that you are?' he questioned rapidly, 'That no man——'

Abruptly Bliss shot to her feet. The paperback, which Quin had returned to her lap, fell to the floor, but she was uncaring of it as she took a few steps forward. 'Sorry to disappoint—when you obviously think I'm a tramp of the first water...' she said stiffly, and would have gone storming away from him then—only suddenly he came behind and placed a pair of restraining hands on her shoulders. Instantly, the whole of her being came alive. The whole of her skin started to tingle, and she was afraid to move a muscle—in case she leant against him.

'I think nothing of the kind, and you know it,' Quin's voice came sharply to her ears. The hands on her shoulders firmed, and then gripped tightly as he said, 'It's just that, with your looks, I'd have thought——'

'What have my looks got to do with anything?' Bliss flared, glad of that spurt of temper which gave her the backbone to pull energetically out of his hold and to spin round to face him. His gaze on her was steady, she observed, but she was pent up suddenly, and rushed on heatedly, to tell him angrily, objecting most strongly to his barely hidden implication that she was a tart, 'Either I decided, way back, that some . . . experiences I could wait for until . . . until the time was really, really right—or I didn't! In my case I did, and I object most strongly to you implying that I'd jump into bed with just about any. . .' She broke off when a roar of a Spanish epithet hit her ears. But she was still staring furiously at him when suddenly his arms came out and he anchored his hands on to her arms.

Then, while stunned, Bliss suffered a moment of weakness from his touch, and found it impossible to shrug out of his hold as she should, 'When did I ever imply anything of the sort?' he roared.

'You did! I'm sure. . .' she began, then faltered, and, if she'd got it all wrong, wanted the floor to open up.

'And you, even with such a wicked temper, I am sure,' Quin took up, his roar quietening to a gentle whisper, 'are much too sensitive.' Bliss stared up at him and, while she had the most awful feeling that she had just made one very big fool of herself, she, sensitive to anything he said because of her love for him, could think of nothing to say. She was still trying to find the strength to back out of his hold, though, when suddenly she saw the corners of his mouth start to pick up. Suddenly, then, in fact, he seemed to be enormously cheerful, when he asked with swamping charm, 'Are you going to show me how much you forgive me by allowing me to take you to lunch?'

'You don't have to entertain me!' Bliss, love a contrary master, found she had resisted his charm to decline coldly.

To her surprise, however, when she wouldn't have been too shaken had he gone all arrogant and told her that in that case she could starve, he remained good-humoured as he replied. 'Do you think I would take you anywhere unless I wanted to?' Her heart burst into sudden happy life—even though she somehow managed to stay solemn-eyed. Then, as she stared gravely at him, 'Would you disappoint a man, Bliss, who, on the pretext of going to his grandmother's funeral, stole time off work to come and get you?'

She couldn't help it, the laughter that had started to bubble in her before suddenly started to bubble up again. And suddenly, gloriously, musically, she just had to burst out laughing. Lying hound—she loved him.

'I'll go and wash my hands,' she announced, her face still alive and amused.

Suddenly then, though, she became aware that Quin, while still good-humoured, was looking at her with a stilled kind of air to him. All at once, then, she was frozen into immobility when his hands on her arms started to draw her closer. 'When did I ever, for a moment, think you always serious?' he asked, and, not waiting for her answer, he unhurriedly bent his head and, gently and beautifully, he kissed her.

Bliss was still trying to come down to earth when, seated beside him in his car, she relived again that brief and beautiful kiss. It hadn't meant anything to him, of course, she knew that—with or without knowing of Paloma—she knew that. But surely, to have kissed her at all, and in that gentle way, must mean that he quite liked her?

They were driving into Pisco when Bliss realised that she would be much better employed in not thinking any more about that kiss. She must not start imagining things in his kiss which just weren't there. Quin had kissed her purely and simply because it had pleased him a little to see her laugh, that was all.

Having parked the car, Quin escorted her to a nearby restaurant, and enquired what she would like to eat. 'Something small—and Peruvian, I think,' she decided.

'You were adventurous once before over a menu, I seem to recall,' he remarked, and added pleasantly, 'Feeling daring again?'

Feeling happy, she wanted to tell him, but of course did not. 'Why not?' she replied, and averted her eyes for fear he might read there the joy she felt just to be with him.

With Quin's help—and she felt wonderful when he chose the same, which endorsed for her what a non-sense love made of you—she ordered something called *papas a la huancaína*, which when it arrived, though a trifle bilious in colour, she felt, had a lovely flavour. Peru had dozens of varieties of potato—she had chosen the yellow one.

'Would you prefer something different?' Quin enquired after she'd sampled a couple of forkfuls of the yellow potatoes with their spicy sauce.

She shook her head, 'I'm enjoying it!' she told him, and, although she'd taken care that he didn't know it, she was enjoying more than just the cheesy, oniony and spicy flavour her palate was detecting.

Quin was a charming host and, to her surprise, soon had her talking on subjects which, when in company of other men of her acquaintance, she hadn't even realised she held strong views on. And that pleased her. With her interest in archaeology occupying so much of her time, she had on the odd occasion wondered if she would turn into the type of person who could talk of nothing else. She silently thanked Quin for the discovery that she had definite views on other matters, and could express them without heat.

Bliss had not thought she wanted a pudding, but suddenly, when she was more hungry for memories to take home with her than for food, she changed her mind and ordered a fruit pancake.

'Do you have time for hobbies?' she asked Quin casually as her pancake arrived. She picked up her fork, and, while she wanted to know all there was to know about him, she all the same didn't want him to gain the impression that she was overly interested, 'When you're not working, I mean,' she looked up to add.

'I'm not working all the time,' Quin told her lightly. Then, with his eyes holding hers, 'I ski, sail,' he began, 'and . . .' Suddenly, he seemed to still. His eyes were still holding hers but it was as if on looking into her large green eyes he had all at once forgotten what he had been about to say ' . . . and, of course, I travel— sometimes managing to mix business with pleasure.'

There were so many things Bliss wanted to say then, among them a light, You must look us up if you ever come to Dorset, but jealousy was gnawing at her heart. 'This pancake's something else again,' she told him while she coped with the realisation that she had nothing whatsoever to do with Quin's momentarily losing his train of thought. Quite plainly, he had not been thinking of her. He'd been looking at her, of course, but in speaking of what he did in his free time his thoughts must obviously have strayed to Paloma Oreja with whom he had most probably last ski'd, and sailed.

'More coffee?' he enquired, as she finished the last of her pancake.

'I couldn't manage another scrap of anything,' she told him. 'If I send another thing down the little red lane I'm sure I'll burst,' she added, and had never loved him more when, amused, he laughed.

'You're a delight,' he told her, and her jealousy was all at once sent on its way, and her cup was full to overflowing.

With her feeling of happiness restored, however, she was again afraid of giving herself away. Glancing from him, she inspected her watch—and then inspected it again. 'Is that the time?' she asked incredulously, and when his mouth turned up at the corners and he nodded, she gasped, 'We've been here nearly three hours!' Suddenly then she was feeling guilty. 'You must be wanting to get back to your office!' she exclaimed quickly, and again saw a smile tug at the corners of his mouth.

'They gave me the rest of the day off,' he said mock-soberly, and, as her love for him rose up within her again, Bliss knew that she needed a few minutes alone in which to get herself back together again.

She glanced about, and spotted the ladies' room. 'If you'll excuse me...' she murmured, and, loving him when he stood up as she stood up, she went off to get herself together.

Quin had settled for their meal when she returned, and she did not sit down again, but, with his hand excitingly on her elbow, was guided back to the car.

'I enjoyed that, thank you!' she saw no harm telling him, and realised that she had been right to thank him that way, for he looked pleased. He then concentrated on extricating them from a sudden traffic snarl-up, and Bliss stayed quiet.

Quin efficiently steered them out of the traffic tangle, and they were soon travelling on the coast road which led back to his home. Bliss tried to keep her feeling of enjoyment with her, and tried not to think of how—certainly within the next four days—she was going to have to leave Quin's home to catch her plane back to England.

But that last thought was starting to prove exceedingly painful, and she was very glad that just at that moment they entered a fishing village where it looked as if the boats had just come in.

'Can we stop?' broke from her in a rush—and when Quin obligingly pulled over she was soon, and for the next twenty minutes, totally absorbed.

The whole of the shore area seemed a complete hive of activity, with people walking, some laden, some not, backwards and forwards. Entire families seemed to have turned out to work on wicker baskets filled with the day's catch from sardines to *corvina*, and there were some fish there which Bliss had never seen before. Expertly, with skills handed down through the generations, she rather thought, fish were gutted, vehicles were loaded, with men, women and children all busy at some labour.

Bliss heard Quin passing the time of day with several of the men as the two of them strolled about, and at one stage sorely regretted not having her camera with her so she could record the marvellous scene. Then she changed her mind about that and was glad that she didn't have her camera, because she had eyes, and she was never going to forget—and in any case to start clicking away suddenly didn't seem right.

'What's this village called?' she asked Quin when, passing a refreshment stall tied together with string that had fruit and Inka Kola—a non-alcoholic mineral drink—and which was all part of the scene, they sauntered back to his car.

'San Andrés,' he replied, and commented, 'You enjoyed that too, didn't you?'

'Did it show?' she asked, San Andrés was full of life, a totally different experience from archaeology and a lovely one.

'In your face,' he replied, and while Bliss made a mental note to be wary of what her expression might reveal when she looked at him, Quin added quietly, 'I'm learning new facets of you the whole time.'

Bliss got into his car, glowing from the feeling that his last comment had sounded complimentary. A few minutes later she was realising that he wasn't the only one who was learning new facets of her. Had she always had the ability to enjoy the simple pleasure of walking through and around a village such as San Andrés when the fishermen returned with their catch? Or was it just that, while totally immersed in what was going on as she had been, she had at the same time been subconsciously aware of observing the scene with the man she loved at her side?

Such thoughts were sufficient to keep her busy until they reached Quin's home. She got out of the car recalling that she had thought her visit to Machu Picchu with Quin had been the best day of her life; but for her there was more than a little something special about the hours she had spent in his company today.

'Tired?' he enquired as they went into the house together.

She wasn't, not at all. 'Pleasantly so,' said she who had done nothing all day but relax. Since, however, she thought that he must now want some time to call his own, she held down the urge to go along to the drawing-room, and latching on to a 'pleasantly tired' excuse instead, told him, 'I think I'll go to my room for a while.' And, although she only ever wanted to be where he was, she smiled her thanks and quickly left him.

For a short time after she had parted from Quin, Bliss lived in a dream world of her happy memories of how well they had got on with each other that day. She had laughed, he had laughed, and not one sour note had been sounded—well, not after she had got angry with him in the summer-house anyhow.

As the minutes ticked by, though, and Bliss realised it was time that she bathed and changed before dinner, so thoughts which she did not want to have began to stir in her head, those thoughts pivoting round the central theme of how Quin must never be allowed to guess at her love for him.

How long had she been here now? she questioned as she went to run her bath. Oh, how the time had flown. Yet, when she had initially been certain that one night in Quin's home was all she was going to endure, here she was still here—it would be a whole week come tomorrow—and she was not *enduring* it, but enjoying it!

Bliss had taken her bath and was dressed in her silk trouser suit when she dwelt on her previously avidly enquiring archaeological self. She was leaving her bedroom and going towards the dining-room when the mortifying thought struck that with her not so much as mentioning her desire to visit Arequipa or Ollantaytambo again; would Quin have noticed that she seemed to have lost interest in her great love— archaeology—and wonder why?

'Pisco Sour?' he enquired as she joined him in the dining-room.

'Thank you,' she accepted, and later took her seat at the table hoping with all she had that he would never guess that she had discovered an even greater love in her life than her hobby.

The first course was brought in and consumed with little in the way of conversation passing between them. They were well into the second course, though, when, while she was fighting with common sense that urged she should tell Quin tonight that she was flying to Arequipa tomorrow, and coping with the fear that if she said any such thing he, with alacrity, would offer to take her to the airport at crack of dawn—oh, where was her pride?—he interrupted her train of thought to comment, 'You're very quiet tonight.'

'Am I?' she answered, and, because she didn't want him to know any of the inner battle she was just then privately fighting, she smiled, and even managed a light laugh as she jokingly suggested, 'Shall I tell you about my job as a librarian?'

She nearly fell off her chair, when, his expression bland, 'Yes,' he replied.

Bliss went to her room after dinner, not having given Quin anything but the sketchiest outline of her work.

She could then only wonder at this nonsensical person she had become; when Quin had suggested she might like to have a look round his library—which he'd said housed tomes in several languages—she had, when there was nothing she would have liked to do better, declared that she had some letters to write. She did not feel at all grateful that, belatedly, some inverted pride should arrive to metaphorically cut off her nose to spite her face.

She slept better that night, however, and awoke the next morning in a positive frame of mind that proclaimed she would that day, with due good manners, of course, snatch at every chance she could to be in Quin's company.

Fearful that he might leave early to go to his office, she had the quickest of showers, threw on some clothes and, swiftly brushing her hair back and securing it with a band, she went, without actually running, to the breakfast-room.

She opened the door, saw that Quin's eyes were on the door as if waiting expectantly for someone—probably Señora Gomez with his coffee, she realised—and, because seeing him was such a joy, she smiled. 'Good morning,' she bade him, and could do nothing at all about the fact that her voice suddenly sounded breathless.

'Have you caught cold?' he questioned sharply.

'You've got your coffee!' she noticed, then, realising he must think her an idiot, she took her seat and replied, 'Not guilty,' to his accusation and then looked across at him. How dear he was to her, she thought, no longer wondering at just what point he had changed from being a monster in her thoughts.

'Then there's no reason why we shouldn't take one of the boats out,' he declared to her astonishment.

'Take a boat out . . .' she echoed.

'You get seasick in a motor boat?' he queried, his eyes on her skin, more of her fine complexion to be seen now that her hair had been swept back from her face.

'Not so far as I know,' she laughed, and could hardly believe her good fortune, even if, as Quin owned the place he worked at, he had no need to ask anyone's permission to have time off. 'Will "they" wear your grandmother's funeral again so soon?' she asked, and positively adored him when his mouth picked up at the corners and a sound of his laugh greeted her ears.

'Did anyone ever tell you that you have the most fantastic bone-structure?' he queried, the words seeming to escape him without his known volition.

'If they did, I missed it,' she replied lightly, and and just couldn't believe that the gods were being this kind to her! 'Er—will we be going very far out?' She thought she'd better try to come down to earth a little.

'You'll need a sweater,' he replied, and informed her, 'We'll take a look at the Ballestas Islands—it might be an idea to bring your camera.'

An hour and a half later, Bliss was of the opinion that it was all too much. Machu Picchu with Quin had been wonderful, the thrill of Nazca with him there beyond words, yesterday with him in Pisco and San Andrés had been terrific, and today—today was quite out of this world!

She had walked along to the jetty near the boat-house an hour ago, just as Quin was manoeuvring a small cabin cruiser out. He'd held her hands as he'd helped her on board and she, of necessity, had stepped close up to him. She had been so close she could smell the clean maleness of him. Needing control, though, she had let go of his hands and moved away as soon as she had been able.

But the adrenalin that had pumped round in her blood had been still there as she'd stood beside him and he'd steered the boat out of his private harbour. And, a short while later, she had swiftly realised why he had suggested she bring her camera. There were birds—hundreds of them. Birds in the air and, as he steered the cabin cruiser near to land, birds on rocks, on cliff-faces, in fact everywhere.

'Is that a cormorant?' she queried excitedly at one stage, pointing and knowing since he had slowed the boat to almost a standstill that they were not likely to come to grief if he took his eyes off where he was steering.

'It's the neotropic cormorant,' he told her, and pointing in another direction, 'Do you see the red-legged species—over there?' For the moment Bliss couldn't pinpoint it. Then her heart leapt up in her body when suddenly Quin moved and put an arm about her shoulders and then turned her slightly. 'There,' he pointed again.

'Oh—y-yes,' she said shakily, and didn't know how he could sound so composed when, at his touch, she was feeling like jelly inside.

He removed his arm when she decided to haphazardly photograph any bird in camera range. In this way she hoped she'd got some superb pictures of oyster catchers, and with Quin helping her out with the names, some Dominican gulls, Inca terns, storm petrels, pelicans and turkey vultures.

Quin cut the engine as they floated close to a rocky cave. 'Listen!' he suggested, and Bliss listened and heard nothing. She listened again, then heard what it was she was supposed to be listening for, a singing sort of 'erooo' sound.

'What is it?' she whispered.

'Some would have it that it's the song of the sea-lions,' he teased, looking into her spell-bound face, 'but...'

'Sea-lions?' she asked, her voice hushed, but suddenly, as she looked at Quin, she had the craziest notion that he was about to kiss her. She forgot completely what they were talking of when, still looking silently at her, his eyes went from her eyes, to her mouth and back to her eyes again. Then suddenly, abruptly, he took his gaze from her and looked to the front—and had no trouble at all in remembering what they had been speaking of when, 'You'd like to see some sea-lions?' he suggested, and, after manoeuvring the boat about, he then steered it through some rocks to where, to her great surprise, she started to make out whole herds of sea-lions.

A short distance later and they were at a section where some of the huge male seals were in the water and were barking loudly while female members of the harem, only their heads visible, bobbed in water close by.

'Did you ever see anything so enthralling?' slipped through Bliss's lips on a whisper of sound, as she turned an excited expression up to Quin. She rather thought as she looked at him that his eyes seemed to be telling her something. For a moment her heart fluttered madly at the ridiculous thought that the slate-grey depths of his eyes appeared to be saying 'You'.

Quickly she gave her attention to the sea. Wishful thinking would get her nowhere, so she had better take her imagination in hand—and right now.

They had been out on the water for about three hours, the time as it had yesterday flying for Bliss, when, as they made their way back, and she had thought that the day could hold no more wonders for her, she suddenly discovered another one.

They were steering close to shore, by rock and sand, when suddenly Bliss caught sight of a mammoth engraving in a steep slope of what she thought was sand. 'What's that!' she exclaimed, and, as Quin slowed the boat so that once more it was barely moving, she was spellbound again.

'El Candelabro,' he replied, and as she realised, now that they were square on, that it was indeed a giant candelabrum shape, Bliss could only stare and stare.

'How old is it?' she wanted to know when, regaining her second wind, she'd realised that it was more carved than dug out of soft sand.

'Theories differ, but some suggest it could be related to the Nazca lines,' he answered, and Bliss was in awe again.

'No!' she exclaimed softly.

'Oh, but yes,' he smiled.

'Heavens!' she sighed. Then suddenly something struck her: that they'd gone the long way out, bypassing this spot. 'Did you save El Candelabro until last on purpose?'

His eyes were laughing when, looking into her eyes, 'Would I?' he teased—and Bliss fell in love with him all over again.

They had a late lunch and, again, because it was all just too much, Bliss spent what was left of the afternoon in her room trying to do the impossible—relive and savour every moment of that glorious morning, while at the same endeavouring to get herself back down on terra firma once more. Quin must like her, mustn't he? He must, surely, to think of saving the staggering sight of El Candelabro until last, as a particular thrill for her.

At dinner that night Bliss began to have second thoughts about whether Quin liked her. She entered the dining-room with her insides all over the place, but, decorum being what it was, she greeted him sedately.

'Good evening,' he returned, and seemed quiet and more than usually lost in his own thoughts throughout the meal, so that Bliss started to feel quite certain that he must be regretting having taken so much time off from his working day.

He did not that evening invite her to have a look round his library after dinner, and, when Bliss had made up her mind to accept should he do so, she went back to her room with a lot on her mind too.

Half an hour later she was still worrying about the change in Quin—he'd been different again at lunch, conversing easily on any subject that happened to come up. Another ten minutes went by, during which she tried to tell herself that it wasn't that he disliked her especially, but that, as a businessman, he must be stuck with any businessman's everyday concerns.

She was in the middle of reminding herself that he had several factories in Lima as well as his business locally, for goodness' sake, when all at once a firm, sharp, single rap sounded on her door—and everything in her went haywire.

She knew in advance that it was not Señora Gomez's knock. Nor was it Leya's sound. And Bliss, trying to keep her features composed, went to the door.

A welcoming smile was desperately struggling for freedom as she opened the door and saw Quin standing there. There was no smile on his face, though, so her smile was sternly repressed. She waited for him to state why he was there, but when he did not the most awful truth dawned on her.

'I'm sorry,' she said chokily, and feeling hurt, humiliated, and wishing herself miles away, she hurriedly turned her back on him in fear that she might break down in ghastly, embarrassed and wounded tears.

'What...?' she heard him question, but his message was understood, for all he'd not said a word. She took more steps into her room away from him.

To her horror, though, while she was still battling against tears, she heard him stride into the room after her. 'I'll pack now,' she quickly told him over her shoulder and took several more hasty steps away from him.

'Pack!' he exclaimed, his voice so close that she knew he was still there—closer than she had thought!

'I should have left a few days ago. I meant t...' She broke off, and was still striving hard for control when suddenly Quin had moved round to the front of her and, as she looked up, she saw that his face was the severest she had ever seen it.

'What the hell are you talking about?' he demanded, his words, the way he said them, suiting his look.

'I...' she began, and, realising that he didn't seem to have the first idea of what was going on in her head, 'I . . .' she said again. Then, 'Haven't you come to ask me to leave?'

'Leave!' he exclaimed, and the severity in his look was replaced by a look of incredulity. 'Why you over-sensitive da...' He broke off, but suddenly, as if, words failing him, he needed to have some action, he suddenly took a hold of her. The next moment she was in his arms. He then lowered his head, and kissed her.

It was a gentle kiss, as his others had been. A giving kiss, but, as his arms tightened about her, there was something else in his kiss too—although Bliss couldn't have said exactly what. All she knew just then was joy as relief washed over her that she, in her admittedly over-sensitive state, had read it all wrong and that Quin had not grown tired of taking time off work to take her about nor did he want her to leave.

'I've wanted to do that all day,' he murmured when, breaking his kiss, he looked down into her shining large green eyes.

'H-have you?' she questioned huskily, and wanted him to kiss her again, and guessed, when he did, that he had read the invitation she extended.

Two kisses were not sufficient for her then, though, for by then she had forgotten any thought of decorum, when it seemed she had loved him for so long, she wanted, needed, the comfort his arms afforded.

With her eyes, her parted lips, showing no sigh of objecting, Quin, a small groan leaving him, gathered her closer to him, and Bliss was in heaven. As he held her near in his embrace, so her arms went round him and she clung on to him.

Passion flared between them as he pressed her closer, yet closer to his manly body. Oh, Quin, she wanted to cry his name, but his mouth had captured hers again and a fire was licking with greedy flames inside her. She held him, her arms around his shoulders as she returned kiss for kiss. And when some while later she found that she was lying with him on her bed, she had barely any notion of having moved.

She gloried in the feel of his hands in her hair, gloried in his touch as he traced tender kisses over the bone-structure he had that morning called fantastic, and knew what it was like to desire a man when, as he traced kisses down to her throat, Quin's hand caressed her body.

'My dear,' he murmured when, the buttons of her dress somehow magically undone, he, by the same magic, slipped her dress effortlessly from her shoulders.

'Quin!' she gasped, and buried her face in his neck, knowing that this was no time to be modest.

His mouth was over hers again when, half lying over her, his hand traced in tender movements to her breasts. She clutched on to him, her body his when she felt the warmth of his touch on her naked skin. How, she had come to be so bereft of clothes—for apart from her briefs she appeared to have nothing else on—Bliss never knew nor was she, just then, interested in enquiring how. She wanted Quin, with all her being, and as he unbuttoned his shirt and let her hands roam freely over his chest, she knew, without shadow of a doubt, that he wanted her.

His hands were at her hips, caressing, pulling her to him and their legs were entwined when he lowered his head to her breasts and kissed the pink peaks he had created.

'You're utterly exquisite!' he breathed hoarsely, and as Bliss opened her eyes and saw that he was looking not at her face, but at her throbbing swollen globes, silken against his manly skin, her face suddenly flamed with colour.

It was at that moment that Quin chose to tear his eyes from her breasts and to look to her face. How he could tell that her high colour was not caused solely by the desire he had created in her, but that a good part of her blush came from this being virgin territory for her, she had no idea. But, all at once, as his hands moved from her hips to tightly grip her upper arms, she saw that he seemed to be fighting desperately for some control.

Looking at him, Bliss was totally bewildered when, his jaw working, he bit off an exclamation in a tongue she couldn't understand and, although a minute before she had been certain that he would lie with her until morning, he then abruptly rolled from the bed and, as if there were a fire in some other part of the house— he rapidly went from her room!

CHAPTER EIGHT

THE thoughts that had kept Bliss company for most of the night were in her head again when, after a fitful night, she awoke again at dawn.

A whole gamut of emotions had assaulted her in her waking hours in darkness. Hope, jealousy, despair, embarrassment. Quin had desired her; whatever else she was uncertain of, she felt she could be certain of that. Yet he had rejected her. Why?

Had she been too willing, too eager? Men, men like him, preferred a conquest, didn't they? Had she made it too easy for him? Feeling suddenly too bruised to live with such humiliating thoughts, Bliss found she had opted for more torture when she wondered whether, if Quin had not changed his mind about making love to her because of her eagerness, the reason he had gone from her was Paloma Oreja? Had he suddenly thought of Paloma, his lost love, and felt some strong and powerful repugnance because he was being disloyal to that love which he bore another woman?

Bliss knew that any chance of going back to sleep was impossible. She left her bed to take a bath and wash her hair, and to wonder, not for the first time—what about herself? For all her high-falutin talk down in the summer-house about how she had decided way back to wait until the time was really, really right—there had been no deciding when she'd been in Quin's arms. It had just sort of—happened.

She left the bathroom, wishing her brain would leave the subject alone. But she hurt, and it wouldn't. She'd been Quin's for the asking, and he'd rejected her and, after the abandoned way she'd been with him, she just didn't know how she was going to face him.

The answer to that evaded her. Then all such thinking went from her mind completely. For as she went to the dressing-table for her hairbrush, she only then spotted something which she hadn't noticed before. There on her dressing table was the paperback book which she had dropped in the summer-house two days ago.

Warm colour rushed to her cheeks as only then did it dawn on her why Quin had come knocking at her door last night. Plainly, he must have been walking in the vicinity of the summer-house, and had found it. What more natural than that he should pop it in to her?

Oh, grief, she mourned; had she not been so uptight about him, she would have said, 'Thank you' nicely, and that would have been an end to it. But no... Unable to cope with anything more just then, Bliss reached for her hair-drier. It proved a ridiculous hope that the noise of her drier would drown out her thoughts.

Her newly washed hair was blow-dried and was healthily shining, and she was dressed in a smart day dress of two-tone green, and there were twelve minutes to go before the time she usually presented herself at breakfast.

Twelve minutes later, and with more courage than the man she loved would ever know about, Bliss left her room. She would not hide—how could she? Love Quin, she did, hurt by him she was, but, rallying what

pride he had left her with, she had no intention that
he, on not seeing her in her usual seat at the usual
time, should wonder why—when it was a foregone
conclusion that he would link her non-appearance at
breakfast with what had happened the last time she
had been in his company.

She reached the breakfast-room door and realised
just then that it had been inevitable that she was going
to feel hurt at some stage. Ever since she had been
crass enough to fall in love with him that had been
obvious. She took a deep and steadying breath, and,
while hoping that perhaps he had breakfasted very
early and was already at his office, she turned the
door-handle.

Quin was not at his office, but was already at
breakfast, 'Good morning,' he bade her civilly,
looking up as she entered the room.

'Good morning,' she replied evenly, and somehow
managed a cool smile as she took her seat. She was
all of a tremble inside, but, provided her hands didn't
give her away, no one was going to know it. *'Buenos
días, señora,'* she looked up to smile at Quin's housekeeper, glad of a third presence when Señora Gomez
followed her into the room.

The housekeeper did not stay longer than to
pleasantly return her greeting and to place coffee and
toast before her. Silence descended on the room once
she had gone, but, reaching for a slice of toast which
she thought would probably choke her, Bliss was
pleased to see that her hands were not trembling.

This was it then, she realised, the moment when she
made polite guest-like noises and spoke, coolly,
calmly, and without emotion, about her departure.
'I——' she began, but discovered that Quin was saying

something at the same time. 'I'm sorry,' she apologised like any well-brought-up person would, and allowed him his say first—which he took.

'I was just about to remark on the Inca ruins of Tambo Colorado—they're said to be the best preserved on the coast.'

'Oh?' Bliss murmured with a show of interest which was not as one hundred per cent true as it once might have been.

'I believe the wall frescoes are quite astonishing,' he informed her, his expression unsmiling.

'Is that so?' she murmured, and found she was asking, 'Is it far from here?'

'About thirty miles,' he answered at once, and, his eyes on her, he asked casually, 'Would you like to go?'

Most definitely not, said her head. 'Er—when?' she asked, when she'd had every intention of telling him that she was leaving—within the next hour or so.

'This morning——' he looked at his watch '—in an hour from now.'

'What about your work?' she questioned, as she fought not to think of the chance he was offering. The chance to spend a few more hours in his sole company.

'What about my work?'

Oh, help me, someone, she wanted to cry. 'You don't have to drive me——'

'I want to,' he cut in, and seemed a shade warmer to her than he had been.

Bliss hesitated, but, as she had been from the moment he'd issued his invitation, she was lost. 'Thank you,' she accepted.

She returned to an immaculate bedroom after breakfast, with Quin's 'I want to' still ringing in her ears. He'd wanted to kiss her all day yesterday, so he'd said, she reminded herself, and look how disastrously that had turned out! Bliss damned that weakness in her that could not say no to him, even as she acknowledged that all she was doing was inviting more hurt.

She had plenty of time before she was due to see him again in which to berate herself for not getting out of there and flying back to England with all speed. Plenty of time in which she began to doubt Quin's 'I want to'. Wasn't it obvious that the only reason he was taking her to this place called Tambo Colorado was because of his respect for his friend, her brother-in-law? With Dom and Erith having to rush to France the way they had, Quin obviously saw it as his duty to put himself at her disposal.

At that point, Bliss started to grow quite cross, and wished more than ever that she had refused Quin's offer and carried on with what she had decided prior to going into breakfast. She left her room a minute before the appointed hour in a not very happy frame of mind and wanted to hate Quin. True, he had never asked her to fall in love with him, and would probably be most appalled by any hint that she had. Though he wasn't going to have a hint—she'd take good care of that.

Bliss joined Quin at his car and got in without a word. It was a fact of life, and she should be thankful, she supposed, that, because he was used to women responding the way she had once he'd melted their bones with a kiss, he would not see anything at all out of the ordinary in the way she'd behaved last night.

Damn him, she fumed, and loved him.

The visit to Tambo Colorado was not a success. Love being a perverse overlord, she found that loving Quin did not stop her from being anti-Quin at the same time. That situation was not helped at all, in that any sign of thawing, or any shade of warmth in him which she had imagined she'd seen at breakfast, had been just that—a figment of her imagination—and no more.

He had not missed that her keenness for things archaeological was lacking, however. She knew that when he enquired curtly, 'Have you seen all you wish to see?' and she realised that when—a lifetime away—they had visited Machu Picchu together, her enthusiasm had been far different than it had been today.

'Plenty, thank you,' she replied shortly; but—although she knew that since he had put himself out for her that morning he deserved warmer thanks than that, the very fact that she could see no warmth in him whatsoever froze her more natural responses.

The journey back to Quin's home was as silent as the outward journey had been. Bliss had nothing she wanted to say to him—he, clearly, returned the compliment.

It was around lunchtime when he pulled his sleek limousine up on his drive, but, when she would have formed the decided view that the next time he saw her would probably be too soon in his opinion, he parted from her with the words, 'I'll see you in the dining-room in ten minutes.'

Bliss had been in her room for five of those ten minutes when she sorted out why Quin had said what he had before she'd walked away from him. She didn't need anyone to tell her that he hadn't suggested he'd see her in the dining-room shortly from any feeling that he couldn't bear to be parted from her, but because, as her host, he felt it incumbent upon him to see that she ate three meals a day.

Again Bliss had to steel herself to go and eat. Quin was already in the dining-room. 'Can I get you something to drink?' he enquired courteously.

'No, thank you,' she replied pleasantly, and realised as she waded through an excellent lunch, which tasted like chaff in her mouth, that that was about the sum total of conversation between them during the meal.

They were at the dessert stage and she was tasting a dish of *mazamorra morada*, which was a kind of purple corn jelly with cherries, apricots and aniseed, when Señora Gomez came into the room with a message for her master. Bliss gave her concentration to her pudding while the two conversed, and she was still finding the purple jelly of much interest when the housekeeper went out, and Quin suddenly addressed her.

'There's a small problem at the factory—if you'll excuse me?' he uttered coolly.

'Of course,' she answered, her smile coldly polite.

His cool glance held hers steadily for a moment, then he was rising from the table. 'Um...' he hesitated. 'Perhaps you'd care to come with me—you could take a look over the plant?'

Had his invitation been in any degree less frosty, Bliss knew she would have jumped at the chance. She wanted to cram in every experience of him, every detail about him, about where he spent some of his day, before she left. She wanted to be able to picture him at his place of work, but... 'That's very kind of you,' she answered him evenly, 'but, actually...' She was talking to the air. Quin had gone.

She waited until she was certain that he had driven away from his home, and then gave up all pretence of wanting her pudding. She left the table, left the dining-room and returned to her room—and could have howled.

She didn't want him playing the dutiful host, in which role he felt he had to keep her amused. Damn him, she railed impotently against that which was not to be—for he would never love her and, by the look of it, didn't even like her. And she began to panic.

The day after tomorrow was the very latest she could stay on here—and despite the pride-denting thought that, for all Quin had made noises to the contrary, he would be dancing a jig when she went, she knew that when it came to it—and perhaps this was the reason why she had been shilly-shallying about leaving—it would break her heart to go.

Feeling more unsettled than ever, Bliss rinsed her face and hands and changed into a knitted shirt and trousers, and applied a smattering of make-up. With part of her, the weak part, she wished that she'd gone with Quin, and she knew a longing to be with him wherever he went. The stronger part of her, however, despaired of the nonsensical person she had become.

Restlessly, feeling near to tears again, she left her room, obeying a sudden restlessness to be elsewhere. Going along a couple of corridors, she halted outside the drawing-room where she had occasionally spent an odd half-hour or so. Suddenly though the thought of trying to sit quietly and leaf through some magazine or other was totally alien. She was too het-up to sit quietly doing nothing.

Within the next five minutes Bliss had left the house and was mooching aimlessly along the shoreline, kicking against fate that when she could be happy here—she knew she could, sublimely—she was going to have to leave.

She had gone quite some way up the beach when she turned about and retraced her steps. But she didn't want to go in yet, so she veered to her right and made for the summer-house.

She had been sitting in the summer-house for no longer than a minute, though, when the memory of how, only two days ago, Quin had come and found her in the summer-house, and had gently kissed her, came flooding back. That beautiful memory, however, was soon clouded by another: the memory of how she had dropped her book, and how Quin had last night come to return it.

Bliss was still squirming with the embarrassment of it all when she realised that her shilly-shallying was over. Suddenly, she knew that tomorrow would see her on a plane bound for England. She had a couple of days left before she was scheduled to depart, it was true, but, since she would not be going to Jahara with Erith not there, and since her zeal to see Ollantaytambo or anywhere else seemed a thing of the past, to return to England was the obvious thing to do.

She realised that she was going to need Quin's help in booking her flight back to Lima, and decided that she would enlist his help at dinner that night. In the meantime, though, there was nothing to stop her from getting her suitcase packed.

With that in mind, Bliss left the summer-house, but only to realise as she entered Quin's house that the

ever-attentive Leya had been keeping an eye on her
activities.

'*Té, señorita!*' she beamed, ever eager to please,
and pointed to the direction of the drawing-room
where Bliss had occasionally taken afternoon tea.

Feeling it would be churlish to refuse—a fifteen-
minute delay would not make that much difference
to her packing—Bliss thanked her, finding a smile,
'*Gracias*, Leya.'

Inside minutes, Bliss was seated in front of a low
table with a tray of tea before her. But the spirit of
restlessness was still in her, and, having poured herself
a cup of tea, she was unable to sit still. Tea in hand,
she paced the thickly carpeted room. Quite obviously
Quin wasn't back yet—oh, why did she have to keep
thinking about him? He followed her, was in her head,
everywhere she went. Was he staying away from home
on purpose because she was there? she even found
herself wondering at one point—and tried in some
desperation to focus her thoughts elsewhere.

She sipped some of her tea, then finding she had
halted near a telephone table she placed her cup and
saucer upon it, and, purely in an exercise to get Quin
out of her head, she lifted the phone off the receiver
and concentrated as hard as she could to see if she
could remember her sister's number.

Erith wouldn't be there, she knew that as she
dialled. She wasn't even sure she was dialling the
correct digits, but by then she was so down and out
of sorts that she didn't care.

Bliss pinned her thoughts on getting ready to say
an English, I'm sorry, I dialled the wrong number,
regardless of the fact that should she have got the
right number and her sister's non-English-speaking

housekeeper answered she wouldn't understand her anyway, when the phone at the other end was picked up and a trace less than confident voice enquired, *'Bueno?'*

There was something most familiar about that voice, and Quin for the moment receded from the forefront of her mind as Bliss enquired, 'Erith?' and was shaken rigid to hear Erith, a plainly relieved Erith, switch rapidly to English.

'Oh, thank goodness it's you!' she exclaimed with a laugh, easily recognising her voice at once. And while Bliss was getting over her shock that her sister was back from France, Erith was going on, 'The phone rang just as I was passing and, expecting to have my ears bombarded with a stream of Spanish, I picked it up.'

'That was very brave of you,' Bliss smiled, recovering rapidly from hearing her sister so unexpectedly. 'Though, knowing you, it won't be long before you start to learn the language,' she added warmly.

'True,' Erith agreed. 'Actually I start my formal lessons next week. Dom teaches me a new sentence every day though—he's a marvellously patient teacher,' she said softly, and sounded so happy, so in love, and so loved, that Bliss felt quite moist-eyed. 'So, what have you been up to?' Erith seemed to collect herself to ask. 'Wh——'

But Bliss didn't want to talk about herself. 'What about you—when did you get back?' she enquired. 'W——'

'You phoned before—while we were out?' she replied. 'We've been into Cuzco——'

'I meant when did you get back from France?' Bliss said more explicitly, and was totally confused at her sister's reply.

'What are you talking about, Bliss?' she asked. 'We haven't been to France!'

'You haven't...' Bliss couldn't take it in. 'But you... I thought...' Helplessly, her voice tailed off.

'You'll have to watch that archaeology, little sister,' Erith laughed, 'I expect you've so thought of nothing else, so seen nothing else and so read of nothing else since you've been in Peru, that you've got mixed up. France was on our honeymoon itinerary, but we came back to Jahara early.' Again that softer tone had entered her voice, but a second later she was saying, 'But you knew that! What made you think we'd left again? We've not spent a night away from Jahara since we got back!'

'I—er...' Bliss was having the hardest time in trying to take in what her sister was telling her, 'Of course— I must be a bit muddle-headed today,' she said lightly, while nothing very clear was going on in her head. It was instinctive in her, however, to not want to do anything, no matter how small, that would put a blight on her sister's happiness. 'I'd somehow got it into my head that Dom's mother was expecting you to——'

'You've got it half right,' Erith butted in. 'She is expecting us, but not until her birthday in October.'

'She's—er—quite well, I hope?' Bliss asked, her head buzzing as she gripped on to the phone and tried to fathom out what in creation was going on.

'She's hardly had a day's illness in her life,' Erith replied, going on, 'Dom rang her yesterday as a matter of fact—she's in excellent health.'

'That's good,' Bliss murmured faintly, and had to believe, though she found it impossible, that Quin Quintero had lied to her about her sister and brother-in-law racing off to see Dom's sick mother in France!

'So what have you been doing? No!' Erith changed her mind. 'I don't want you to tell me over the phone. You can tell me in person when you get here. You *are* coming to see us, aren't you?' she questioned in that tone that said she'd expect an exceptionally good reason if she wasn't.

'How about tomorrow?' Bliss, the fog in her head none the clearer, asked.

'We'll meet you at Cuzco airport. Where are you now?' she suddenly stumped her by asking.

Bliss didn't like lying to her sister—but she had never been in love before. And, even if it looked as though Quin was a swine of the first water, a rat, a lying toad, somehow, with her love for him total, that love went hand in hand with loyalty. 'I'm near Nazca,' she heard herself lie.

'I knew you wouldn't miss Nazca!' Erith laughed.

'I'll give you a ring tomorrow when I know what time my plane gets in,' Bliss told her, and after a minute or two more, she quietly put down the receiver, feeling totally stunned.

She stayed that way for quite some minutes, still not being able to take in what was so apparent—that if Erith had not been to France, if Dom's mother was in excellent health, then Quin—had lied!

When, whichever way she looked at it, the answer still came out the same—Quin had definitely, but definitely lied to her when he'd told her that Erith and Dom had left Peru for France—Bliss's anger came roaringly alive. And she had never been more glad of it. Without that anger, she felt she would have folded, for, all too clearly, Quin was so contemptuous of her that he thought he could tell her anything he wished if it suited him.

Why it should have suited him to tell such an outrageous lie was beyond her just then. It had bothered her that she had lied to Erith, but what about Quin's lie? His *blatant*, *unashamed* lie to her! He'd known full well that her sister and brother-in-law had no immediate plans to leave Jahara.

It was at that moment that her pride suddenly took over. She had, she fully admitted, been appallingly weak in the pride department—but not any more. In the next second, choking back a wayward sob, she was racing from the drawing-room to her bedroom.

She had that night intended to enlist Quin's help in booking a flight for tomorrow. Like hell, she sniffed, and was suddenly outraged. She wasn't waiting for tomorrow, or tonight either; she was getting out—right now!

Extracting her suitcase from a large cupboard in her room, Bliss tossed it to the bed, her thoughts charging on to how she would get through to Señora Gomez somehow, once her packing was done, that she would like a taxi straight away.

Bliss was furiously flinging things inside her case and had her back to the door as she went from wardrobe to the bed. In her fury, she was deaf to faint sound, and totally ignorant that a tall, well-built, slate-grey-eyed man had opened her door and, having taken a step forward, was now standing watching her.

Damn Quin Quintero, she silently railed, damn him to hell, she couldn't wait to be done with him. If she couldn't get a flight out today, then she'd jolly well spend the night in a hotel in Pisco rather than spend another night under his roof. How dared he! Damn his nerve! Who did...? She turned, caught sight of the man standing near the door, stopped dead, and then beamed all her hate vibes in his direction.

'Thanks for knocking!' she hurled at him violently, and was unconcerned at the sudden aggressive thrust of his jaw at her tone.

If she had angered him, though, he controlled that anger very well when, his grey eyes pinning her flashing green ones, he remarked, his look alert, vigilant, 'You—seem—to be in something of a hurry.'

'You could say that!' Bliss snapped, hating him some more because, heaven help her, just seeing him weakened her.

'You're—thinking of leaving?' he questioned evenly.

'Ten out of ten for observation!' she threw at him sarcastically, and just could not believe her ears at his next comment.

'And what if I'm not ready—to let you leave?' he questioned abruptly.

Of all the nerve! 'In a word,' Bliss fired hotly, 'tough!' Oh-oh, he didn't like that, she could tell from the way his hands clenched at his sides for a moment. She turned to get something else from the wardrobe, but couldn't avoid seeing the intelligence in his eyes that showed he was trying to weigh up what had put her in this furious mood.

But she just had to pause to look at him again when, his audacity endless, he had the utter gall to ask, 'How do you think you're going to get to Lima without my help?'

It was patently obvious to her then that his way of repaying her for her remark was to try and make it 'tough' for her. But she took that sort of treatment from no one, and was very much up on her high horse when, her chin tilted an arrogant fraction, she told him stonily, 'Should I be going to Lima, I've no doubt whatsoever that I'd make it without your help. But——'

'You're not going to Lima?' he cut in, picking out what she'd slipped up on—for she hadn't worked out yet whether she wanted him to know where she was going.

'No, I'm not!' she replied coldly, and then wondered why the heck she should be coy about it. 'As a matter of fact,' she continued, 'I'm going to Cuzco.'

Bliss knew, the instant the name 'Cuzco' had left her, that Quin had promptly worked out what all this was about. For, suddenly, there was a stilled kind of waiting look about him, and when, after a few seconds of just staring thoughtfully at her, he then queried, 'Cuzco?' Bliss decided to play along with him.

'To be more precise, a place called Jahara,' she told him coolly. 'I've a sister living there,' she further informed him. 'I rang her a short while ago.' She saw his eyes narrow, but he was giving nothing of his thoughts away. Her control of her cool tone, though, was rapidly fading, but she managed to find a tart note when she fairly hurled at him, 'Given the gravity of her mother-in-law's illness—she got back from France earlier than I would have thought!'

Long seconds passed as Bliss glared silently at Quin and he, his expression still giving nothing away, stared back at her. Then, when ageless moments had ticked by, 'It seems,' he broke the silence, 'that I've some ... explaining ... to do.'

And you can't get much more magnanimous than that, she fumed. But as nerves started to bite, so her anger against him, against the effortless ability he had to weaken her, flamed into life again, and sparks were flashing in her eyes once more when, 'What the *hell* makes you think I'm remotely interested?' she exploded spiritedly.

'There's no good reason why you should be,' he replied shortly, his jaw jerking, and added, to make her jaw drop, 'But you're going nowhere, believe me, until you've heard me out!' Bliss opened her mouth, ready to tell him what she thought of that, even though there was that in his tone that there was no arguing with. Then she discovered that she had left her argument too late for, all proud Peruvian, he was going on to command, 'I'd be obliged, *señorita*, if you'd join me in the drawing-room.'

With that, he turned and went, and Bliss, staring after him in disbelief, was left wondering how, she, it seemed, was suddenly the one in the wrong!

CHAPTER NINE

FOR all of two minutes Bliss stared at the empty doorway and was certain that she'd see Quin Quintero in hell first before she'd take one single solitary step to 'oblige' him by 'joining him in the drawing-room'.

Another minute went by during which she fumed against his nerve in daring, actually *daring*, to make it seem as if she was the one in the wrong when he was the one who had been lying in his teeth from way back. Probably before Cuzco, she railed, remembering that they had been in Cuzco when he'd fed her that foul lie that her sister and her husband had flown, post-haste, to France.

Sixty more seconds ticked by with no let-up in her fury, but when another thirty seconds was over Bliss was starting to form the view that she wouldn't mind seeing Señor-lying-Quintin Quintero for five minutes so that she could tell him exactly who she thought— no, *knew*—was in the wrong.

The wretched hound, had he played her for a fool! *Why* he had, she hadn't yet fathomed, but she doubted that there was any explanation that would... Her thoughts broke off as she remembered how he had, reluctantly, it was true, admitted, '...I've some...explaining...to do,' and she took a few involuntary steps towards the door.

Then she halted. It was something, though, she supposed, that the lofty devil seeming *willing* to explain, and she took a few more steps that brought her to the open doorway.

Oh, to the devil with it, she thought in a sudden flush of irritation, and, even though she was certain that he of the 'You're going nowhere until you've heard me out' school couldn't keep her in his home by force, her steps picked up speed and she was suddenly storming angrily to the drawing-room.

He was standing watching the door as she got there. She thought for one brief moment that there seemed to be an edge of strain about him. She swiftly cancelled that notion, however, realising that while she had suddenly started to feel quite shaky inside, he was looking quite cool, calm and collected.

'Come and take a seat,' he instructed, his voice even as he pointed to one of the two settees in the room.

Bliss saw no reason why she should thank him for the invitation, but because her legs, infuriatingly, were all at once feeling all 'jellyish', she, with her head tilted at an uppity angle, went over to a softly padded settee. Seeming in no hurry, she elegantly lowered herself on to it, noting absently that the table nearby, which had not so long ago held a tray of tea, had been cleared.

Then, sitting straight-backed, she raised her head, and raised her eyes to the tall, grey-eyed man who was surveying her carefully. 'If you could be brief,' she addressed him, 'I'd like to be on my way within the next ten minutes.'

'What I have to say may take longer than that!' he clipped, and at his curt tone Bliss, while wondering what on earth he had to say that could take longer than ten minutes, realised, with a pang of hurt which she did not need just then, that Quin no longer liked her.

If he ever had, her pride prodded, for how could any man be so contemptuous of you to lie the way he had—and at the same time like you? 'Then perhaps,' she drawled, amazed how pride could make a brilliant actress of her, 'and since I don't want to be suffering from a stiff neck tomorrow, you wouldn't mind sitting down too—or shall I stand up?'

She had no need to stand she saw, for Quin was moving. Even if he was throwing her a look that said she, with her uppity manner, wasn't his favourite person just then, he moved to take his ease on the settee opposite.

He was leaning back, quite relaxed, with one arm placed carelessly along the top of the settee when, after a few moments' pause, he looked across at her, and told her sharply, 'I owe you an apology.'

If that was the way he was going to make it, then Bliss didn't think it was going to be much of an apology. It could have been, of course, that his tone had been sharp because he was nervous, but Bliss knew that it wasn't that. She had never seen Quin as a man who would grovel either, so this sharp and to-the-point apology was the best she was going to get, she realised.

'Well, three cheers for you,' she snapped sourly. 'Am I to be grateful that, apparently, you agree that you're the one in the wrong, and not me?'

'You were never the one in the wrong, Bliss,' he surprised her by suddenly stating, his tone all at once so much warmer that she was again instantly weakened.

'So I'm an angel!' she erupted crossly, annoyed that he could, just by a change of tone, make such a nonsense of her. 'So why lie?'

'Because . . .' he began and broke off, and although Bliss wasn't believing it, she could have sworn that he actually *did* seem nervous. She knew she had imagined that, however, when, a few seconds later, he resumed, and stated unequivocally, 'You were unwell. You needed to rest—you know, if you're honest, that that's so.'

'You're a fine one to talk of honesty!' she exploded, but, when he stared back, innocent and unblushing, she tossed him a belligerent, 'There wasn't any need to lie on that account.'

'There was,' he amended categorically.

'How?'

'You'd exhausted yourself and were refusing to admit it. It seemed logical to threaten to inform your sister that you weren't well.'

'You blackmailed me!' she hotly laid another charge at his door. 'You emotionally blackmailed me!'

'And you called my bluff,' he replied. This the first she'd heard that he had been bluffing! 'You said that you'd go and see your sister the very next day.' He took a long drawn breath, then, 'That,' he said, 'wasn't what I wanted either.'

Bliss confessed herself lost to know what it was he did want then, as she said, 'So you told me that Erith and Dom had gone to France . . .' She broke off, her brow wrinkling slightly. 'I could have rested if I'd gone to stay at Jahara for a day or two—Erith would have seen to that.'

'But—I didn't want you to go to Jahara.'

'You didn't?' Bliss questioned slowly. She knew her reasons for not wanting to stay at Jahara for any length of time—she'd no intention of trespassing on Erith and Dom's honeymoon—but were Quin's reasons the same? 'Why?' she just had to ask.

'Um—everything—snowballed,' he answered, which to her was no sort of an answer. He had her staring at him, her heartbeats erratic though, when, looking straight into her large green eyes, 'I—wanted you in my home,' he suddenly, and abruptly, revealed.

Hastily Bliss averted her gaze. What he'd said had sounded so—possessive somehow. Yet, as she got herself more together, she was swiftly remembering how, last night, when she had been his for the possessing, he'd rolled from her bed and rapidly left her. So, whatever else she might be confused about, she knew for sure that Quin hadn't brought her to his home in order to get her to go to bed with him.

But, having remembered the ardent way in which she had responded, she was at pains, should he be thinking any such thoughts too, to hurriedly change his mind in case he might be thinking that she was any—once-kissed—clinging female.

'You wanted me in your home and were prepared to blackmail me to get your way!' she angrily erupted, and had not finished yet as, aggressively, she stormed on, 'It irked you that, having decided I should recuperate in your home, you found that I wasn't some obedient *señorita*. Pure male chauvinism reared its bossy head, and——'

'Male chauvinism had nothing to do with it!' Quin rapped sharply, but by then Bliss had got herself wound up, and she wasn't ready for him or anyone else to put her down. 'Not much it hadn't!' she flared.

'You lied when it became obvious that there was no other way of getting your own way.' She barely realised that she had lost so much control when, 'You've had a down on women ever since Paloma Oreja finished with you...' She had raced on hotly, only to stop, appalled, as what she was saying suddenly hit her. Oh, how *could* she have been so careless of his feelings to say what so dreadfully, so cruelly—and, yes, so jealously—she had just said? 'I'm s-so sorry,' she apologised at once. 'I didn't mean... You made me so angry, but...'

'Think nothing of it!' Quin retorted stiffly, and, while she was no longer sitting back looking relaxed, his arm left the padded back of the settee he was on, and he was leaning forward. 'I may have remarked on your formidable temper before,' he threw in, not looking in the least afraid of it, 'but, to keep the record straight, it was not Paloma Oreja who finished with me.'

Bliss stared at him, somewhat shaken, she had to admit, as her intelligence went to work. 'You—ditched her?' she asked, unable to see what else he could have meant.

'I'd have perhaps phrased it differently——' he shrugged '—though it amounts to the same thing,' he conceded.

'But—you said... You told me...' she pushed on, forgetting completely what was at issue here in the light of what Quin was now telling her. 'You told me she'd finished with you,' she said finally, unexpectedly having had the devil's own work in trying to remember exactly what, in relation to Paloma Oreja throwing him over, he had said.

'When did I ever say anything of the sort?' Quin challenged her to tell him.

'You said that—you'd come close to getting engaged!' Bliss just then remembered.

Then she realised that she'd got that wrong when Quin, clearly a man with instant recall, corrected, 'What I actually said was that, for a while, one of us believed it would come to that—you, Bliss,' he informed her, 'decided for yourself that I was the one to believe it.'

'But—it wasn't you?' she questioned, her eyes huge as it started to dawn on her that perhaps he hadn't been in love with Paloma—after all!

He shook his head. 'She was getting serious—I never was.'

A ton weight seemed to lift off Bliss at his statement. Quin was not, and never had been, in love with his ex-girlfriend! Warmth and gladness filled her being, but, of course, there was no way that she was going to let him see how his news had affected her. 'Take a girl to bed and see where that will get you!' she told him with some asperity—and could have groaned out loud that she might have directed his thoughts back to what had taken place between them in her bedroom last night.

She was very grateful then that, for all his right eyebrow twitched upwards the merest fraction, he did not comment on the forward way she had been, but commented, 'I didn't bed her—she was holding out for marriage.'

Bliss very nearly swallowed. Indeed, she had a hard job not to at the thought that Quin couldn't pin anything like that on her. Lord help her—she'd have freely given herself to him last night had he not rejected her.

'Though, in point of fact,' he went on, when for the moment she was lost to find her tongue, 'matters between myself and the lady never got that heated.'

'Oh?' Bliss murmured, not much of a contribution, she had to own, but what with realising that Quin was not in love with Paloma Oreja, she was all over the place inside that Quin—a very private man, she had realised—should open up and tell her what he was telling her now. As if it was of some importance, somehow, that she should recognise how things had been for him.

She had dismissed any such fantastic notion, however, when he went on, 'Having that Monday said a permanent farewell to a woman who, to my amazement and without that sort of encouragement from me, was talking in terms of announcing our engagement, I was more than a little off the whole opportunist female population.' He paused for a moment or two, and then slowly added, 'And that was before, on that same Monday, I entered the dining-room of my hotel in Lima, and at once saw the most beautiful flame-haired woman piling on the charm for one of my—plainly not impecunious—countrymen.'

'For your information,' Bliss burst out hotly, suddenly having the same instant recall as he, any fluttering in her heart region at the compliment to her beauty negated by what else he had said, 'I was not piling on the charm! It didn't matter to me one way or the other if Señor...' she broke off, having difficulty in remembering the man's name, 'if Señor—Videla,' she remembered, 'had money or if he didn't! And I resent——'

'Quite rightly too,' Quin, astonishingly and immediately, agreed with her, and when Bliss, silenced in mid-fury, coldly looked at him, he quietly stated, 'Your charm is, I've discovered, a natural charm.'

Bliss wasn't sure that she didn't swallow then, for Quin's charm, when he cared to use it, was something else again. 'Señor Videla's young son, as it happens, was in hospital in Lima, and, even though the boy was making progress, his wife was too distressed to come down to dinner that night. She was asleep when he left her to——'

'I'm sure everything you say is true,' Quin mildly butted in when it seemed that her temper was about to flare.

'Well . . .' she sniffed, and looked briefly down into her lap. 'You'd got a real down on me before we ever spoke to each other,' she abruptly looked up to remind him sharply. 'I saw you the next day and you looked through me!'

'Did you not return the favour?' he enquired.

Bliss ignored that. 'And the first time that you did speak to me it was only to snarl something about why didn't I look where the hell I was going? In fact whenever I saw you, be it at breakfast time or whenever, you couldn't have made it plainer that you'd a down on me.'

'You seemed to be bowling over all who came within range of your lovely green eyes,' Quin replied, and added, 'I confess, having just disentangled myself from one beautiful but calculating female, that I was in no mood to invite a similar situation by passing so much as a solitary pleasantry with the next beautiful woman I came into contact with.'

'Me?' Bliss enquired, while at the same time hating that part of her that made her put the question.

'Even more beautiful, I should have said,' he answered, his words sounding matter-of-fact, and not at all like flattery. 'I obviously recognised that you spelt trouble before I so much as knew who——'

'Trouble!' she cut in, ready to erupt, for all she could not help but be thrilled that he thought her more beautiful than Paloma Oreja.

'Oh, yes,' he replied, 'and flirtatious, too——'

'I wasn't!' she denied strenuously.

'Or so I thought at that time,' he finished what she hadn't given him a chance to finish.

'You changed your mind—er—later?' she queried, snatching at calm.

'Of course,' he stated, though he admitted, 'But that was after Dom de Zarmoza's phone call asking me to call on you to see if there was anything I could do to assist you in a country you were unfamiliar with.'

'You didn't consider that it might be me when you promised to take me to dinner?'

'It didn't so much as cross my mind,' he owned. 'That hotel in Lima was large enough for me to have missed seeing the sweet and gentle Miss Carter Dom spoke of. When he told me how wrapped up you were in your hobby of archaeology, the idea was instantly born that you must be some bespectacled plain and scholarly woman who was probably unaware that a world existed outside antiquity. It was something of a shock to discover that the woman who'd got half the men in that hotel falling over themselves to speak to her was the same Miss Carter I'd come to take to dinner,' he ended.

It was at that moment that Bliss discovered that she had been quite mesmerised by what he had been saying. But, as it suddenly came to her that she had been exceedingly angry with him, but did not seem to be angry any more, she searched for, and found, a strand of aggressiveness. 'Serves you right!' she told him shortly.

'I couldn't agree more,' he replied, which totally flummoxed her.

That was until she all at once remembered what she was doing there in his drawing-room. Then she could hardly credit that, when she had been so furious, she had allowed him—and she was sure he'd done it on purpose—to draw her away from the issue at stake.

'We seem to have drifted off the point!' she at once decided to get straight back to it—only it seemed that Quin had different ideas.

'We'll come to why I did what I did in a moment,' he decided authoritatively, with not so much as a smile on him. 'What I'm trying to get you to see,' he went on a trace less bossily, 'is that, with my experience of some women being ready to sell their souls for an affluent catch, you—were something else again.'

'Is that meant to be a compliment?' she questioned waspishly, and, her sensitivity ever over-active where he was concerned, she could have sworn she glimpsed a suggestion in his strong face that he was a touch unsure of himself.

'I knew, when it came to it, that I'd explain this badly,' he said on a long drawn breath.

'You sound as if . . . as if . . . you'd always meant to explain?' she took up.

'Believe me—I'm not a natural born liar,' he replied. 'Indeed, when . . .' He halted. Then he seemed to make a determined effort. And there was not so much as a glimmer of a suggestion that he was unsure of himself then, when he continued, 'To go back to the beginning, back to when Dom rang. Clearly he's so in love with his bride that other women and what they look like are just not registering on his consciousness. So, without thinking to mention your Titian hair or marvellous complexion—which would have given me a very good hint of who Miss Carter might be—he instead spoke only of your hobby, sweet disposition and how, because you'd been so ill a few months back that they'd nearly lost you, his wife, your sister, couldn't help being anxious about you.'

'I didn't want worry about me to spoil Erith's honeymoon!' Bliss declared in some disquiet, and had her fears soothed straight away.

'Dom would soon convince her that you were all right,' he stated unhesitatingly. 'He knew I was in Lima, and at the first sign that something was troubling his wife he got in touch. Having given my word that no problem you had would be too small or too large for me to assist you with—I dined with you.'

'And realised that I didn't need your assistance in any matter.'

'So you said at the time,' he nodded, but was silent for a moment or two. Then, as though choosing his words carefully, he went on, 'And which I believed—but which didn't explain why, on overhearing you making arrangements to fly to Cuzco, I should, later that day, make a point of checking which flight you were booked on—and arrange to be on the same plane.'

'You . . . I . . .' Bliss stared at him, shock from what he had said seeming to have turned her brain numb. 'I asked you if you were in Cuzco on business!' she remembered, as her brain woke up. She then also remembered that Quin had cuttingly replied that it was none of her concern. 'You're n-not saying that you went to Cuzco purely because you overheard me book a flight there?' she questioned in astonishment.

'I'd no reason to take that flight,' Quin replied quietly.

'But . . .' She couldn't take it in, but as she speedily searched round in her head for an answer, she suddenly found one. 'Because you'd promised my brother-in-law——'

'I believed I'd done all that was required of me on that score,' Quin replied, somewhat to her amazement when she thought of all that had followed. Her eyes were glued to his unswerving steady look when he added, 'I was still wondering what I was doing altering my schedule and going to Cuzco when the plane took off. But I was no nearer knowing when, after we landed, you asked if I'd business in Cuzco. How could I tell you, when I was still wondering myself what the hell I was doing there?'

'Good—heavens!' she said faintly, and, whether she wanted it or not, something came over her then that made her intrigued, and impatient to hear more. She had lost all sight of her intention to leave as soon as she could when she queried, 'Did you—er—ever find out—why you'd caught that plane to Cuzco, I mean?'

Several seconds ticked by as Quin scrutinised her interested expression. 'Oh—yes,' he stated softly, paused, and then went on carefully, 'I came close to discovery the very next evening when I shared your table at dinner. Your expression was alive as you told me how you'd spent your day, your eyes ashine with wonder from all you'd seen that day.' Briefly, he looked away from her, but his slate-grey-eyed look was on her when, his voice even, he told her, 'I started to be charmed by you at dinner that night, and I knew then, when you said that you hoped to take a look at Machu Picchu the next day, that I—wanted to be there with you when you did.'

'Honestly?' Bliss exclaimed on a strangled kind of note, 'I thought . . . You said . . . Charmed?' she just had to question. His answer was to have her staring at him incredulously.

'I started to—fall—under your spell, my dear,' he quietly replied.

Her throat went dry, and all she seemed capable of doing was to repeat words which he had said. 'M-my—spell?' she choked.

'It had started before then, of course,' he murmured, 'but only when I knew that I had to go to Machu Picchu the next day too did I acknowledge that you, rather than the chance to see Machu Picchu again, were the reason I would go.'

Bliss very nearly queried, 'Honestly?' again, but, with her heart thudding, her insides all a-tremble, she strove to find what remnants of calm she could. 'I thought . . . Er—you . . . I'm sure . . .' She broke off, so many bitty, half formed sentences were going through her head. With some difficulty, though, she at last got herself more together and, not wanting Quin to think that she had gone completely to pieces because he should say something of a most pleasant nature to her, she managed to complete a whole sentence. 'Did you—enjoy Machu Picchu?' she queried.

'With you, it was like a new discovery,' he replied, to warm her heart. 'In fact,' he went further, his eyes alert on her, 'I made other new discoveries that day.'

'Oh,' she murmured, and wanted, needed more than anything that he should go on. 'What—sort of discoveries?' she invited, her voice suddenly husky. 'When?'

'When?' he took up. 'When I held you in my arms exhausted after your attack of coughing. The discovery? That I wanted to protect you, to watch over you. To care——'

'Oh!' she exclaimed in sudden panic, and felt all at once afraid—though of what she knew not. Without thought she was off the settee, on her feet and, turning, was taking a few agitated steps to widen the gap between them. But Quin could move quickly too, and he had left his settee and was right there behind her when she halted.

'I've alarmed you, Bliss?' he questioned urgently, his voice suddenly thick in his throat. 'You don't want to know that...' He broke off, his hands coming to her shoulders, whether he knew it or not, and gripping her tightly.

'I'm...' she murmured huskily and wanted to tell him that she was quite enchanted by what he was saying but that yes, she was alarmed, alarmed that he might see just how much she did want him to care. 'I—was that why you lied to me—ab-about Erith...?'

'Partly,' he owned. 'Though, more particularly, I couldn't bear the thought of you going away from me.' Bliss was suddenly stock still in his hold. Again his hands clenched on her shoulders, but she didn't mind.

She was unaware of breathing, unaware of anything save that there was some stupendous meaning in what Quin seemed to be saying. 'You—wanted me—n-near?' she questioned at last, her words a mere breath of a sound.

'For ever,' Quin said firmly, and slowly, though Bliss was not resisting, he turned her round to face him.

'For—*ever*?' She raised large green eyes to his.

'My dear,' Quin breathed, the warmth in his look as he gazed down at her, making her swallow hard, 'Have I managed to cover so completely what else happened to me when I held you in my arms at Machu Picchu? Have you no idea at all of how much I—love you?'

Without knowing it, her hands came up and clutched at him. 'You—l-love...?' It was no good, she couldn't get the words out.

But the fact that she had clutched at him rather than pushed him away seemed to be of some encouragement to the man who gently placed his arms around her, and studied every nuance in her expression.

'I knew it that marvellous day,' he confirmed, his look steady.

Bliss looked up at him and couldn't believe what was happening. But it was. She therefore strove her hardest to use her intelligence, because this—to be loved by Quin—was the fulfilment of all her dreams. And it just couldn't be—could it?

'Is—th-that why you were so—cross with me the n-next day?' she stammered out the only opposition she could think of.

'Cross?' he repeated, but there was a hint of a smile trying to tug at the corners of his mouth. 'How could I ever be cross with you, my little one?'

'You were—bad-tempered when—in that hotel in Cuzco I didn't want any breakfast.'

'I was *concerned* about you, my dear,' he gently corrected her. 'You'd overtired yourself, and weren't looking well.'

'You—were—er—quite bossy,' she told him without heat as she still struggled to get her head together after what he'd said. Did he love her? Could he love her? Oh, dear lord, she wanted him to—so much!

'How else should I be?' he questioned, his arms secure bands about her. 'You were exhausted and planning on climbing all over Ollantaytambo that day. I had to protect you—from yourself.'

'Which is why you invented that story about my sister and her husband being in France?'

Tenderly he placed a kiss on her brow, then, gently, he laid a beautiful kiss on her mouth. 'When your lips are parted like that they're quite irresistible—did you know that?' he asked, and when, dumbly, she shook her head he moved her with him back to the settee which she had sprung up from. 'You'll allow me to sit close by you while I explain how, when hearing the lengths my friend Dom went to to gain his love, I was certain that nothing in this world would ever have me so enamoured that I would ever resort to such tactics?' Quin now had her comfortably seated next to him on the settee. 'But what do I find,' he questioned, 'but that, within a very short space of time, when you stubbornly refuse to give me the time I wanted with you that, I've actually resorted to telling lies to prevent you from going away from me?'

'You—er—could have come to Jahara, too,' Bliss, with what thinking ability he'd left her with, pointed out. 'Dom's a friend of yours. He'd have——'

'All true, of course,' Quin agreed. 'But you'd already revealed that you'd no intention of intruding on the honeymooning couple for any length of time. Which meant, since I was determined I should be near you, that I should again have to follow where you led. Don't you see, dear Bliss,' he asked, 'that while it was important to me then that you didn't know that I'd fallen in love with you, it was quite plain that if I followed you around much more you'd soon begin to wonder why? I couldn't have that,' he said wryly with a smile that made her heart turn over. 'So the only other way in which I could have you near the whole time was the obvious one.'

'To take me to your home,' Bliss filled in—he had just repeated his love, hadn't he? She hadn't imagined that 'I'd fallen in love with you,' had she?

'I wanted to look after you. In my love and desperation, I'd already resorted to lying. Though in actual fact I'd forgotten that Dom's mother lived in France until you asked me if she was ill. From there,' he revealed, 'everything miraculously started to fit in well.'

'I flew to Paracas with you,' Bliss documented.

'And I fell more and more in love with you with every passing day,' he breathed softly. 'Then,' he resumed, 'I started to have nightmares about how it would all end when I confessed, as confess I knew I soon must, what I'd done. Would you ever speak to me again, much less return some of my love as I wanted, when you knew, your visit to Peru at an end, that I'd deprived you of seeing your sister whom it's clear you do love?' There seemed to be a suspended kind of hush in the room when Quin, his hands holding hers in a suddenly tense grip, asked, 'Am I deluding myself totally, Bliss, in thinking that you aren't the kind of woman to exact your revenge for my dishonesty by allowing me to reveal what is in my heart unless you—have some small caring for me too?'

She swallowed hard. 'You—truly love me?' she asked with what voice her husky throat would allow.

'With my life,' Quin replied, and asked imperatively, 'Am I, as I began to feel last night, more to you than any man has been to you before?' Bliss looked at him and knew he was referring to the way she would last night have been his—had he not left her. She realised then that she'd little chance of hiding from him what she felt. And then, 'Please, Bliss,' he urged, his jaw working, the whole of his expression showing the strain he was under, 'Can you not tell me what lies in your heart?'

At that, when he seemed in such an agony of suspense, Bliss found her voice, choky though it sounded. 'L-love,' she whispered. 'Love.'

'For?' he questioned tautly.

'You. All f-for you,' she stammered shyly.

For long moments after the words had left her Quin just looked and looked at her as though—like her minutes previously—he was having the hardest work in believing what she was actually saying.

Then, 'You're sure—that you love me.'

'Oh, yes, I'm sure,' she told him shyly, and, since he seemed tense still. 'I—er—l-love you,' she told him tremulously.

What it was he cried exultantly in Spanish she had no idea. Then she ceased to care for, tenderly, almost reverently, he took her in his arms. 'My dear love,' he whispered, and gently he kissed her eyes, then gently he kissed her mouth. Then, most gently of all, he tenderly drew her close up against his heart. 'When?' he asked, and, while Bliss was in a rapture of happiness to be in his arms, her sensitivity to him was nevertheless working to let her know what he was asking.

'When did I know—that I loved you?' she asked shyly, and felt his firm hold tighten, as she admitted, 'It had been staring me in the face for days, but I refused to see it.'

'My stubborn darling,' he murmured against her hair, but insisted, 'Go on.'

'We'd been to Nazca,' she obliged, 'and it was so fantastic, I just couldn't get over it. And then, when we were back in Pisco, you kissed me—and from then on I could barely think about my hobby at all. I knew that night that I was in love with you.'

Gently, tenderly, Quin kissed her. 'Since Sunday?' he questioned. 'I've endured agonies, uncertainties, in my love for you—and you've known since Sunday!'

'If it's any consolation,' she said softly, 'I've hurt too.'

'No!' he exclaimed as if there was no way he would tolerate her being hurt. 'You've been hurt by me!'

'And by my imagination,' she replied, and, when he moved her slightly so he could look down into her face, she confessed, 'I realised that I loved you, but thought you were in love with Paloma Oreja.'

'You were jealous!' Quin asked in surprise.

'Well...' she said lamely, and looked a touch ashamed so that he laughed, a marvellous sound to her, and pulled her close to him again.

'You've no need to be jealous of her or any other woman,' he murmured as he placed a loving kiss on her ear. 'I know how painful that emotion can be— I'm sorry. Forgive me for causing—if inadvertently——'

'You've known jealousy over someone?' Bliss asked, the knowledge that Quin loved her so new that she was still a little insecure.

'Over you, only you,' Quin at once assured her. 'No other woman has ever had that power over me. Only you, my dear love,' he breathed.

'Truly?' she questioned.

'Believe me, until I knew you, I'd no knowledge of that monster, or how powerfully it can rage.'

Her lips parted in surprise that he had made acquaintance with that ferocious and unrelenting demon. And, as though unable to resist, Quin kissed her parted lips, then, his kiss deepening, he gathered her more closely to him, and, as Bliss wound her arms around him, long satisfying minutes passed.

She knew that her skin was flushed when, again gently, he pulled back from her. 'You're—er—making it very difficult, my dear,' he said, his voice gravelly, and unlike his normal voice, 'for me to remember that your brother-in-law trusted me with your sweet self.' Quin's adoring eyes were on her pinkened cheeks when he gave in and kissed her briefly once more. 'Now,' he said as he pulled back, 'what were we talking about?' Bliss was so mesmerised by him that she had no idea, so she was quite glad when he remembered and stated, 'Ah, yes, jealousy—that plaguer of men.'

'And women,' she added, and had to ask, 'But who were you jealous of?'

'Any man who dared to look at you, I've discovered,' he replied without hesitation, and itemised, 'I felt the first pin-prick of jealousy that night we dined together in Lima.'

'Back then?' she questioned, her eyes shooting wide. She loved him all over again when he smiled, and nodded.

'Naturally I didn't acknowledge it as jealousy at the time, just irritation at your bad manners in flirting with the two males who nearly burst a blood vessel to get you to smile at them as they entered the dining-room.'

'I was just being polite to them,' she thought she should mention.

'Of course you were,' he agreed, 'but I've discovered that there's no reason to jealousy. It gave me hell over Ned Jones—you're sure you and he are just good friends?' he asked, a touch fiercely, she rather thought.

'Believe it,' she laughed softly, and suddenly realised that she felt much more secure about Quin's love than she had done. So much so that she voluntarily told him, 'Oh, I do love you, so very, very much, Quin Quintero.'

'My love,' he breathed, and a few more minutes of silence ensued, during which he planted tiny loving kisses all over her face. 'I once told you you were a delight——'

'I remember—did you mean it?'

'I meant it then, and I mean it now,' he stated. 'Can you doubt it when, because I wanted to be free to witness your enjoyment, to watch your changing expressions, I purposely got someone else to pilot us over the Nazca lines?' Bliss was staring at him in utter amazement when he went on, 'Or when back at Pisco, as I looked down at your alive and glowing face, my heart suddenly rose up. I just couldn't stop myself from kissing you,' he declared.

'Oh, Quin,' she breathed.

'One kiss, my love, was never enough,' he told her softly. 'Is it any wonder that, afraid of giving myself away, I should turn from you to grasp for control.'

'I never guessed!'

'You were not supposed to,' he teased, though his tone was markedly altered when he went on, 'Did I need to get my head back together after that! I deliberately kept away from you for the rest of that day.'

'You had some business commitments,' she remembered.

'More lies,' he confessed. 'I needed some time away from you to try to sort out what I was going to do.'

'It was so bad?'

'And how,' he replied. 'You'd that morning told me that you didn't want to keep me from my work—plainly not knowing that, with thoughts of you and how I might have little chance with you, you were keeping me from my sleep, my food, and, I was beginning to think, driving me insane.'

'Oh!' she sighed. 'Darling Quin.'

'Thank you for that,' he smiled, and, clearly liking the way she had called him 'darling', he kissed her and then, gaining control, continued, 'I decided that I was going to have to play it cool from there on. And told myself that it suited me quite well when you didn't appear at breakfast at your usual time the next morning. I took myself off to my office—but inside the first five minutes I put through a call to Señora Gomez to see if you're all right.'

Bliss could hardly believe Quin was telling her all this, but by no means, did she want him to stop. 'Er—to borrow your phrase—go on,' she pressed softly.

'Señora Gomez assured me that you were at breakfast and seemed quite well,' he willingly did so, 'but still the same I found that I couldn't settle. It was around noon when I just had to come and check for myself that you were all right.'

'You found me in the summer-house,' Bliss remembered.

'I did—but only after searching for you everywhere and, in doing so, realising just how desolate life was going to be if, should I not be able to think of a way of making you stay, you left.'

'I'd no idea . . .' she gasped.

'Can you believe that I, with my decision to play it cool from there on, should suddenly hear myself inviting you out to lunch?' he smiled, and made her eyes shine with happiness when he reminded her, 'That was the wonderful day we had lunch in Pisco and returned via San Andrés, where I thought my heart would burst for love of you.'

Her large green eyes soft and loving, Bliss stared at him. 'Really?' she asked huskily.

'Very really,' he breathed. 'Never shall I forget the look of rapt, innocent pleasure on your face as we strolled around and about that fishing village.' For some seconds then, as if overcoming some strong emotion, he just held her quietly against his heart, then he resumed, 'Can you blame me for wanting to take you out the next day, yesterday, and have you all to myself?'

'We went round the fabulous Ballestas Islands,' she smiled, 'and I thought everything was wonderful.'

'I was with you—what more could I want?' Quin inserted.

'Yet . . .' she began, but hesitated.

'Yet?' he prompted.

'That night—last night—at dinner, you were quiet, withdrawn somehow, and I was certain that you were regretting having taken so much time off from your working day.'

'Forgive me,' he apologised, 'I'd a lot on my mind.'

'Your work...?'

'Work nothing,' he grinned. 'Apart from a slight hiccup today that required my attention, my business runs very well without too much attention from me. I put in an appearance at my office the first couple of days you were here because, having wanted you in my home, I was having difficulty in learning to cope with the happiness from just having you here. I needed space, a place where I could get myself together—learn to hide my emotions. By last Friday, though, you seemed to be much recovered from the fatigue that you'd endured, and—chiefly because I wanted to be with you, I admit—I couldn't even think of any good reason why I should deprive myself of your company.'

'You took me to a museum and...' she threw him a teasing look '...allowed me to swim elsewhere than in the pool.'

'Both Señora Gomez and Leya had strict instructions to watch over you when I was not around,' he laughed. Though he was not laughing when, seriously, he went on, 'I came close to panic that Friday.'

'Panic—you?' she asked in surprise.

'You were talking of leaving,' he replied. 'I couldn't have that, nor was I going to have that but, since I'd observed for myself a certain stubbornness in your nature, how was I to stop you?'

'You rogue,' she told him lovingly. 'You dangled that museum, archaeology, like a carrot. Not to mention allowing me to swim in the sea.'

'I shan't ever forget that,' he replied. 'I thought you were in difficulties and raced over—only to find myself in difficulties once I held your half-naked body in my arms. I was fighting like hell for control when you pushed me away.' He paused then, 'Did I imagine it, Bliss, or—were you "physically" aware of me too?'

'Do I have to tell the truth?' she teased.

'Aren't all fibs, white lies, evasions and downright lies over between us from now on, my dear?' he questioned simply.

'Then you didn't imagine it. I've never felt like that before,' she at once confessed.

His head came down and it was as if it had been too long between kisses, for Quin kissed her long and lingeringly. Then he again put some space between their two bodies, giving her a rueful look, and, as though searching his mind for what they had last been talking of, he paused, then proceeded, 'In no time at all, dear Bliss, I realised that I'd got myself into a fine predicament.'

'Over me?' she wanted to know.

'Who else but you?' he replied, his eyes going down to her mouth at her sudden mischievous look. 'Daily I grew afraid that you were going to tell me you were leaving—but I wanted more time with you, I couldn't let you go.'

'I've been ready to tell you for several days now that I was going,' she confessed.

'My senses didn't play me false, then,' Quin remarked.

And Bliss just had to tell him, 'Only each time I'd made up my mind to leave, you suggested we go somewhere and . . .' She broke off. 'Did you do that on purpose?' she questioned, suddenly astonished.

'You're getting very good at reading me, Bliss,' he grinned, and her heart turned over with her love for him.

'Is it any wonder that I just didn't have the strength to turn down your suggestions—but had to give in to the chance to be with you a little while longer?' she asked.

'I'm glad,' he said without pretence, and Bliss snuggled close up to him.

'So I wasn't the only one who was off my food over love,' she murmured.

'Was what why you weren't eating?' He seemed surprised.

'I ate most of the time,' she laughed, and Quin laughed, a wonderful sound, and they looked at each other, sharing each other's joy.

'It's perhaps as well that I didn't confess all of this last night as I intended,' he murmured then, his warm gaze transferring from her eyes to her parted lips and back to her eyes again.

'When you came to my room?' she questioned, and as the word 'intended' registered, not waiting for his answer, she exclaimed, 'But you came to return my book!'

'Your book was my excuse,' Quin corrected, and amazed her when he went on, 'I was in something of a state of nerves, and needed some small idea, object, to break the ice when I came—intending to explain if I could my deception about your sister being in France when she wasn't.'

Staring at him wide-eyed again, Bliss, while having difficulty in crediting that Quin had been so nervous that he'd needed a cover, trusted him completely. Even as she gasped, 'You—nervous?' she trusted him.

'I've never been so unsure of myself in my life,' he owned. 'I'd been prepared to do anything I had to to keep you near to me, but as the time drew near when you were scheduled to leave my country I began to grow quite desperate to know how to keep you here longer.'

'Oh, my dear!' she sighed softly, realising then that while she had been going through an agony of hurt Quin had been going through a quiet hell of his own.

'Remind me to tell you how much I love you some time,' he took time out to smilingly tell her. Then he went on, 'I knew I had to confess my lie, but the time was going on with no time seeming the right time. I couldn't bear the thought of having to say goodbye to you, yet felt quite certain that were I to tell you that I brought you here—told that lie—from love, that you would scorn such love.'

Bliss leaned forward and, gently, she kissed him. 'I'd no idea,' she whispered softly.

'You weren't meant to,' he smiled, and held her close as he told her, 'Last night, at dinner, I got so uptight—at the thought that any word I spoke of having brought you to my home under false pretences would see you walking out on me—that I could barely say a word.'

'Was that when you made up your mind to come to my room?'

'No, that was later, after dinner. You'd left the dining-room and I took a walk as far as the summer-house. It was there that I found your book, but when

I faced that another long night had to be got through, and that I wouldn't see you again before breakfast—I decided enough was enough.'

'You came to see me...'

'And promptly lost sight of all my rehearsed phrases when you seemed to think that I'd come to ask you to leave. It was then that I found I was doing what I'd wanted to do all day. I was holding you in my arms. We kissed, and, for a brief while—heaven was mine.'

'But you—er—l-left,' she reminded him, a certain shyness there for all she thought that there was nothing which she couldn't discuss with him now.

'Sweet love, what was I to do? I wanted you, you in your untutored way wanted me, I knew, but your blushes, your shyness, suddenly got through to me and I knew that I had to go while I could.'

'Because you didn't think it was right that we—when—er—you hadn't explained anything?' Bliss questioned.

'That,' Quin agreed, 'plus the fact that while I could still believe I hadn't broken my old friend's trust in that you had been exhausted and had needed to rest—hence my bringing you here—the trust he had placed in me would have been broken had I stayed.'

'I think,' Bliss murmured softly, 'that you must be the most honourable man I've ever met.'

'So,' Quin grinned, 'do I.'

It was good to laugh with him, to feel the skin of his face against the skin of her face as they hugged and sat close. 'Remind me to tell you how much I love you,' she sighed happily.

'Daily,' he insisted, but continued, 'After leaving you, I didn't know where the hell I was. I spent the worst night of my life, still feeling shaken by the way you'd responded to me, while at the same time I grew more desperate that, with the hours fast disappearing, the only thing you might feel for me when I did come clean would be loathing that I'd deprived you of the chance to see your sister while you were in her new country.'

'If it's any consolation, I didn't sleep much either,' Bliss inserted softly, and they kissed in mutual love and understanding.

'I hope your head was clearer than mine by this morning,' Quin murmured, a smile there in his voice.

'You hadn't decided what you were going to do?'

'All I knew for sure as dawn arrived was that with you about to leave any day now I was going to spend every minute I could of this day with you.'

'Is that why we went to Tambo Colorado?'

'Of course,' he replied, and admitted, 'It was a disaster, wasn't it? All the while I wanted to tell you I loved you, when at the same time it just didn't feel right. What if I scared you off? It was then that I began to sift through yet again every word and everything else that had taken place between us.'

'Did you come to any fresh conclusions?' Bliss wanted to know.

'Hope tried to struggle through,' Quin answered. 'It was then that I began to think that if you'd reacted to any of your men friends in the way you'd responded when I'd held you in my arms, then no way would you still be a virgin. So that had to mean that you had *not* reacted, or responded to any man that way. Which in turn—dared I hope—had to mean that I was ''special'' in some kind of way.'

'Oh, dear,' she laughed lightly, 'I blew my cover didn't I?'

'Not quite,' Quin answered, 'I hoped, but wasn't quite believing. Then, after lunch I was at the factory, when my thoughts ever on you, and I began sifting again and playing back our morning at Tambo Colorado over in my mind. At first it was a source of regret to me that when any archaeologically minded person would think Tambo Colorado quite something, you had barely seemed interested.'

'You—noticed.'

'I'm aware of most things you do, my dear,' he breathed. 'What, I then began to wonder, had happened to dull your enthusiasm? Or had something happened not to particularly dull your enthusiasm, but to supersede it? Had you perhaps found something of greater interest? When I started to link those thoughts with memories of the way you'd been with me last night, the way you'd responded, hope that you might be interested in me, that I might be "special" to you, started to spiral. Before I knew it, I was in my car speeding to you.'

'You found me packing to leave,' Bliss smiled.

'First of all I had an agitated Leya meet me as I got out of my car telling me that she'd seen the *señorita* running from the drawing-room to her bedroom looking very upset. Can you wonder that I came into your room without thinking to knock?'

'I'm glad that you did!' she laughed joyously.

'That,' he said decisively, 'makes two of us.' Again they kissed, and all was silent for some while, then Quin pulled back and seemed to be making a great effort to pin his thoughts elsewhere. 'Er—why did you ring Jahara, by the way?' he asked. 'Did you think Dom and your sister would be back?'

Bliss shook her head. 'I couldn't get you out of my mind. I dialled Erith's number purely to make myself concentrate on something else. I had the shock of my life when Erith answered.'

'You told her you were here with me in Paracas?'

'I—er—told her I was near Nazca. I didn't mean to lie,' she added quickly. 'I—it just ... I'm supposed to be going to Cuzco tomorrow!' she suddenly remembered.

'Do not worry, my loyal little darling,' Quin smiled, seeming to instantly know the way it had been. 'I'll tell both your sister and Dom that you've been staying in my home when I see them.'

'You're going to see them?'

'We're both going—tomorrow.' He moved her so that he could see into her face, and she looked up to the warmth in his slate-grey eyes as he said, 'You'll want them both at our wedding, won't you?'

'W-wedding!' she exclaimed huskily, her heart once more hammering away inside her body.

'Of course wedding,' he replied firmly. 'I knew I wanted above everything to marry you that day I was telling you of my married brothers—both with sons. I'd been about to add how very pleased I was about them because it gave me the freedom to enjoy a permanently happy bachelorhood. But, it wasn't true, and hadn't been since Machu Picchu, and all I knew then was that the only way I could be truly happy was if I was married—to you.'

'Oh, Quin,' Bliss sighed, and was gently kissed before the man she loved seemed determined to have a more binding answer.

'Will your father mind, within months, losing his second daughter this year?' he asked.

'Within months—this year!' Bliss felt hardly able to breathe.

'You're not going to make me wait to claim my bride, are you?' he asked, his steady look unwavering. Bliss knew then that he was serious about not wanting to wait.

Suddenly a lovely smile broke from her. 'I wouldn't dream of it!' she declared softly. In the next moment, she was close up against his heart again.

HARLEQUIN
Romance®